Douglas Hyde

The Story of Early Gaelic Literature

Douglas Hyde

The Story of Early Gaelic Literature

ISBN/EAN: 9783743419377

Manufactured in Europe, USA, Canada, Australia, Japa

Cover: Foto ©Andreas Hilbeck / pixelio.de

Manufactured and distributed by brebook publishing software (www.brebook.com)

Douglas Hyde

The Story of Early Gaelic Literature

THE STORY OF EARLY
GAELIC LITERATURE

BY

DOUGLAS HYDE, LL.D., M.R.I.A.

(Ꝺn Chꞃꞵoibhín Ꝺoibhínn)

President of the Gaelic League. Author of "Leꞵꞵꞃ Sgeul�.
ꞡeꞵċꞵꞵ," "Beside the Fire," "Love Songs of Connacht," &c.

"Ogygia too, in Greek, is equivalent to 'Insula Perantiqua,'
that is 'Very-ancient Island.' And a fitting name is that for
Erin, because it is far in the past that she was first inhabited,
and because perfect is the exact knowledge which her Shanachies
possess of the records of her ancients from the beginning of the
ages, generation after generation."

—*From the Irish of* Seꝺꞇꞃún Céiꞇínꞡ.

London
T. FISHER UNWIN
PATERNOSTER SQUARE

Dublin	New York
SEALY, BRYERS & WALKER	P. J. KENEDY
MIDDLE ABBEY STREET	BARCLAY STREET

MDCCCXCV

Caiṟsim an Leabhaiṟín ṟeo
Maṟ buan-chuimhne aṟ mo ċáiṟvib
Seumaṟ Mac Aovhaṡáin Saṡaṟc, aṡuṟ Euṟeb D Mac
Cliabaiṟ ollaṁ Diaḃaċca.

TO THE MEMORY OF MY LATE DEAR FRIENDS

THE REV. EUSEBY D. CLEAVER,

OF DOLGELLY, NORTH WALES, AND

FATHER JAMES KEEGAN,

OF ST. LOUIS, U.S.A., WHOSE LIFE-LONG, FAR-REACHING,

PERSISTENT AND UNSELFISH EFFORTS

TO STEM THE EVER-INCREASING ANGLICISATION

OF OUR RACE,

HAVE EARNED THE WARM GRATITUDE OF ALL THOSE

IRISHMEN

WHO DO NOT DESIRE TO SEE OUR ANCIENT IRISH NATION

SINK INTO A WEST BRITAIN.

PREFACE.

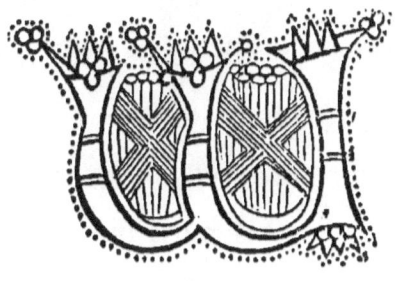HEN Trelawny the friend of Byron and Shelley, who himself played so romantic a part in the revival of Greece, afterwards surveyed dispassionately the almost miraculous emergence of that nation from the blackest night into the warm day, he thus pointed the moral as it appeared to him: "no people," he said, "if they retain their name and language need despair." That pledge of liberty, that guarantee of nationality, Ireland like Greece possessed—possessed even when Trelawny wrote—but possesses no more.

Whoever takes the trouble to acquaint himself

with the history of the life and death of our language
and literature, which after a luxuriant and steady
growth lasting from the very dawn of Irish history,
has, almost in our own day, been stricken and de-
cayed like some secular elm, blighted by disease
within a single season, can hardly avoid being im-
pressed with the instability of human tongues. Not
that the history of mankind is not full of such
instances, but it has nothing of the kind to show
in modern times so startling, so wholesale, and so
rapid, as this sudden extinguishing of one of the
finest, most perfect, and best-preserved of the great
Aryan languages. It has gone—this most important
of those units which go to constitute the nationality
of the Clann-na-nGael; gone, as a day in the late
autumn sometimes gives way to night with scarce any
intervening twilight; gone with its songs, ballads,
poems, folk-lore, romances and literature.

It is at this literature, which flourished so long
and was extinguished so suddenly, that I desire to
glance in this little volume; it is, roughly speaking,
the literature of the entire Irish race down to the

year 1600, of ninety-nine hundreths of the race down to the year 1700, and after that of an ever-diminishing portion of it, which was attenuated to about one-half at the time of the Great Famine, after which death-blow, if the Celts did not quite "go with a vengeance," as the *Times* boasted, their literature, songs, traditions, and language did.

It would be obviously impossible within the limits of this small book to attempt anything like an exhaustive catalogue of the literature produced in Irish, or of the names of Irish writers. Such a catalogue and such a list, if carefully compiled, would be of the greatest value, but would perhaps hardly be suitable for the more popular series of the "Irish Library." I shall here merely attempt to give some general idea of our literature and its history, touching lightly on its more salient features and most striking names, and illustrating it by a few extracts from the original in prose and verse, which may serve as samples of Gaelic style.

The moment the English reader embarks on the sea of native Irish literature, he finds himself in

absolutely unknown waters. It is not merely that
the style, the phraseology, the turns of speech, the
entire metrical system, are as unlike English as
though the whole of Europe lay between the two
countries, but its allusions are to things and times
and events and cycles and dynasties, strange and
unknown to him, and he thus finds himself suddenly
launched into a new world, whose existence was by
him perfectly unsuspected. He is beset on every
side by allusions which he cannot understand, similes
he cannot grasp, and ideas which are strange to him.
Of course, after a little familiarity with our manuscript literature, he will learn that such a term as
"descendant of the race of Lopus" means a vulgar
upstart, that an "Ossian after the Fenians" is an
ancient left alone in this world by kith, kin and
contemporaries, that the "plain of Felim" is another
name for Ireland, that to be descended from the
"three Collas" is to be of the Ultonian race, in other
words, a Northern, that the "sons of Ir and of Ere-
mhóin" mean the Irish stock, and so on. Nor is this
all. The now familiar topographical system of coun-

ties will not avail him in the least. He will have to
learn that Conn's Half and Eóghan's Half mean
Connacht-and-Ulster and Munster-and-Leinster respectively, he will have to acquaint himself with the
hitherto unheard-of districts of Bregia, Oriel, Hy-
Many, the Decies, Ofaly, Breffny, the Paoracha, and
the rest. The O'Conors of Connacht he may have
known before, but will he recognize them under the
title of the Síol Murray; the MacDonnells of Antrim
may be familiar to him, but will he know them under
the patronymic of the Race of Colla Uais? Will
he understand that the tribe of Eóghan Mór represent the MacCarthys of Munster, or know that the
Cinel Conaill are the sept that gave to the Irish
race the great Red Hugh? If he learns to speak
Irish he will never hear of anything less than the
"*five* provinces," he will find Ireland called not
only Eire but Banba and Fola, names he never
heard before ; and an Englishman learning our
language and embarking on our literature might
nearly as well find himself in Russia. This lends
to Irish literature a peculiar value and a great en-

chantment, for its fibres to the latest day of its life
were twined deep down in the soil of Ireland,
knit inseparably to the ancient history, mythology,
topography and romance of the island. But it also
had this disadvantage : that the moment the Irish
language and literature ceased to be the preponder-
ating language and literature in Ireland, they died
away with unparalleled rapidity, because they were
so utterly unlike, so diametrically opposed to what
men were now beginning to learn and to study.
Had there been any resemblance, had there been
the least community between the two, they might
have lived somewhat longer side by side. But as
things were, those who had once got hold of English,
in most cases, refused to undergo the mental labour
of cultivating the mother tongue, and the very general idea that to speak Irish "ruined one's English"
helped to prevent a generation of bi-linguists from
arising. And this was in one way natural enough,
for there are some dozen and a half of *sounds* alone
in the Irish language which are not in the English,
and which no speaker of English or of the Romance

languages only, could master without trouble. Let us glance at the course of the two literatures side by side.

Before the beginning of the seventeenth century no work of any size had ever been undertaken in Ireland by any Englishman, with the exception of Spenser's *View*, Hanmer's *Chronicle*, and Campion's *Historie.** The seventeenth century itself which saw such terrific and annihilating blows struck against the Gael, was nevertheless a most productive one in literature, and during at least the first half of it, the

---

* Spenser's *View* was written in 1596, but was not published till 1633. Campion's *Historie of Ireland* was written twenty-five years earlier, but was only published in the same year as Spenser's *View*. I am not sure that Hanmer was published before 1633 either, in which year Sir James Ware put all three into print. Stanihurst does not fall within the scope of my statement, for he was an Irishman. His *De Rebus in Hibernià gestis* saw the light at Antwerp in 1584. Fynes Moryson's *Itinerary*, of which about one-third is dedicated to Ireland, was first published in 1617, but was written long before, though probably not in Ireland. The first English translation from an Irish prose work was, as far as I know, Conal Macgeoghegan's *Annals of Clonmacnois* made about 1627—a work which I hope will see the light before the end of the year. The first translation of an Irish poetical work was O'Kearney's metrical version of O'Dugan's *Kings of the race of Eibhear*, a most wretched affair.

Irish tried hard to keep abreast of the rest of Europe. Many of the great writers in this century used Irish exclusively, as did Keating, the O'Clerys, Duald MacFirbirs, O'Mulloy, O'Hussey, and a host of others. Some, again, of equal literary fame super-added Latin to Irish, as though foreseeing that the native language might not be cultivated in the future as it had been in the past, and hence Ward, Colgan, O'Sullivan Beare, Father Lynch, Florence O'Mul-conry, Father White, and Roderick O'Flaherty wrote either in Latin or in both Irish and Latin. There were even then, however, men of English descent but Irish birth, men of the Pale, rising up, in whom English blood and Irish nurture contrasted curiously. Ussher and Ware were the most distinguished of these, and they, though not unfamiliar with Irish, as far as was necessary for literary purposes, made use in their writings only of Latin and English. Towards the end of the century some even of the Catholic Irish are found using English, as Peter Walsh, Nicho-las French and Hugh O'Reilly, but these were all without exception men who had lived much at court, and were rather politicians than authors. After that came Molyneux, born in Dublin, son of a Cromwellian, and he was the forerunner of the Swifts and Grattans and Floods, who in the eighteenth century dwarfed for the first time in Ireland the Gaelic race. Of course it was not difficult to dwarf them under the conditions of that age, since all the best Gaelic families of the four provinces in whom lay the educated brain of the nation, had been rooted out, slain, or banished, and all those who were left were deprived by law of almost every chance of bettering themselves, and above all had their life-possibilities stifled at the birth by being deprived of education. And as the eighteenth century, filled for the Irish nation with pain and shame, agony and degradation, dragged itself slowly through, all eyes were fixed on our brilliant Grattans and Floods, on our House in College Green, on Charlemont and his Volunteers, and the Gaelic race seemed to be effaced from the earth. But it was not so. During all this time the dwarfed, unnoticed, unheeded Gael, the bone and sinew of the Irish nation, the fathers of those men who outside of North-East Ulster to-day *are* the Irish nation, had a system of education of their own, a arge if furtively-produced literature, and a race of poets, who in one thing at least, in the exquisite delicacy of their ear, and in the rhythm and music of their language far surpassed even the palmiest days of their predecessors, and produced the most sensuous attempt at conveying music in language that the world probably ever witnessed. With the nineteenth century came eclipse. The first half of it, up to the Great Famine, found the bulk of the nation still Gaelic, and produced several poets in Connacht and Munster, the latter half little or nothing, and it would seem reserved for this coming century, unless the most vigorous effort of which our race is capable be at once made, to catch the last tones of that beautiful unmixed Aryan language which, with the exception of that glorious Greek which has now renewed its youth like the eagle, has left the longest, most luminous, and most consecutive literary track behind it of any of the vernacular tongues of Europe.

As one might be prepared to expect, a literature so

widely cultivated and of so long a growth, branched out into many different directions and embraced as wide a diversity of style as English itself. There is certainly no one leading feature which one could venture to call "Irish" more than another. Yet it is common of late to hear of English authors who have "caught the Irish style," of a poem or ballad being "quite in the Irish style," and so on. The truth is that there were dozens of different literary movements in the language, each characterized by a something of its own. There is the style of the older sagas and annals, which is distinguished by its brief, plain, intelligible and straightforward sentences. There is the style of the later saga, declamatory, thunderous, adjectival. There is the style of Keating, smooth, complex, Latin-like, the sentences unrolling themselves slowly and passing on to their stately and polished close. There is the style of the bardic schools, which I might denominate, if it were not a bull, as condensation running riot, and perhaps if any style more than another deserves the appellation of Irish it is this. We have the sensible style of the seventeenth century poets who were the first to break themselves loose from the fetters of the schools. We have the style of our later poetry, nebulous with Swinburnian diffuseness, almost cloying with five-fold Swinburnian melody. We have the semi-epic style of the Ossianic epopees, a happy medium between bardic condensation and lyric diffuseness. Any attempt to reproduce these modes in English must always prove completely inadequate, because it is likely that there never was a language whose literature so largely depended upon the sound of its vocables as the Irish, and hence, important as the getting of Irish literature into the English tongue must be, it is of far more importance, from a literary and aesthetic stand-point, to diffuse a knowledge of the tongue itself in which it is written.

Everyone knows now, or ought to know, that Irish is, like Greek, Latin and Sanscrit, a pure Aryan language, and a highly-inflected and very beautiful one also. Had it not been for Aughrim, the Boyne and the Penal laws, it would undoubtedly now be the language of all Ireland, and have probably produced

a splendid modern literature. The numerous conti-
nental scholars who have studied it (and who now
freely admit that Old Irish ranks near to Sanscrit in
importance for the philologist) all speak of it in terms
of highest praise, and one German has said that had
it continued to be cultivated down to the present
day, it would—flexible as it is—have been found as
equal to the wants and emergencies of modern life
as German itself. As it is, the language has not received even a trace of fair play, not having been
spoken in law courts, camps, or colleges since the first
half of the seventeenth century, up to which time it
had been cultivated with more assiduity than almost
any other European tongue, and was quite able to hold
its own with any language in the world. During the
eighteenth century it ceased to be spoken or written
by scientists and men of learning, or to put things
more plainly, the men who spoke it were unable to
produce men of science or learning since they were
by law deprived of education. This being so, the
Irish language has not kept abreast of the last century
and a half, and has not, like other languages, produced
vernacular names for scientific, political, banking,

engineering, or mathematical terms. That it could have done so with the greatest ease is certain, and since the small attempt made within the last few years to rake a few live cinders out of the expiring Gaelic fire, Irish has been found to supply quite readily most of the terms required by this *fin de siècle* life, thanks to its power of forming word-combinations,* in which it scarcely falls short of Greek and German.

The causes which brought about the extinction of

---

* Thus such words as *rúin-chléireach* for secretary of a meeting, *gal-charbad* or *cóiste-iarainn* for train, *bóthar-iarainn* for railroad, *teachtaireacht-teinntigh* for telegram (or *sgeul-ar-bhárr-bata*), *dá-rothán* and *tri-rothán* for bicycle and tricycle, have become quite natural as it were, to the members of the Gaelic League who make it their rule to converse in Irish. These phrases which may now be regarded as stereotyped, mean literally *secret-clerk, steam-chariot,* or *iron-coach, iron-road, lightning-message,* or *story-on-top-of-a-stick,*—this last an ancient and proverbial phrase probably first used about Ogams cut on sticks planted upright in the ground—*two-wheeleen, three-wheeleen,* etc. In one respect Irish is both weaker and stronger than German, for it only takes kindly to word-combinations, when the first word is a monosyllable. This of course diminishes its power of expression, but vastly increases its gracefulness. The Gaelic League (rooms, 4 College Green, Dublin; Secretary, Mr. John MacNeill, annual subscription, 5s.) is now doing its utmost to keep our language, Ireland's noblest heritage, alive in those districts where it is still spoken. But it is a matter not for individual effort but for a nation to move in.

our language over so large a part of the country may be classed under several headings as political, religious, and social, and were, in every respect, very complex. To attempt to trace them out—as I sincerely hope they shall some day be traced—would be sure to arouse violent animosities at present, and would be a task unsuited for this brief preface. One cause for slighting the Irish language is the grotesque misconception that there is nothing to read in it. One of the stereotyped, unvarying, never-failing objections to its study in the mouth, not only of West-Britons but of many good Irishmen, is to be found in the assertion that it contains no literature. How in the face of all that foreign scholars have done and are doing, in the face of the *Revue Celtique*, in the face of the *Gaelic Journal*, in the face of the end of the nineteenth century such a popular fallacy still obtains wide-spread credence, is astounding. That it should be believed in England, Scotland, Wales, even Europe, that the Irish had no literature is easily conceivable, but that Irishmen themselves—the unique and predominant glory of whose race, if they only knew it, is their literature—should believe they have none, is as remarkable as the action of literary men of note highly-esteemed in Ireland, who until recently deliberately discouraged all attempts at its cultivation

This little sketch of the history of our literature is intended as a sort of answer to those who still repeat that there is no literature in Irish ; but the best answer would be to ask them to walk into the Royal Irish Academy in Dawson Street and look at the long rows and piles of Irish MSS. on the shelves there, requesting them to remember that as many more may be seen in Trinity College, the British Museum, Maynooth College, the Bodleian, and else-where, so that if they were all printed they would probably fill 1,200 or 1,400 octavo volumes, perhaps even more.

Only three writers of English* have attempted to

---

* It has no doubt often been done by Gaelic writers whose works and very names are lost. We know that at least one such great compilation was made about 1660 by the last hereditary historian of Lower Connacht, Duald MacFirbis, who says in his yet extant book of Genealogies that it required a large work to give the names merely of the Gaelic writers with the titles of their tracts. The loss of MacFirbis's work is an irreparable calamity.

give any account of the more important works contained in this vast literature, they are Bishop Nichol-
son, Edward O'Reilly, and Eugene O'Curry. The
first of these was an Englishman, created Archbishop
of Cashel, and—like Bishop Bedell—one of the excessively few out of the hordes of the English clerical
place-men of the seventeenth and eighteenth centuries
who attempted either to understand the country and
its people, or to give back something for all they took.
His *Irish Historical Library*, published in 1724, is
a very painstaking attempt to give a catalogue of
Irish historical books and manuscripts, quite surpris-
ing, considering the circumstances under which the
bishop compiled it.

In 1820 O'Reilly, who, three years before this,
had published his great Irish Dictionary, produced
his "Chronological Account of nearly four hundred
Irish [Gaelic] Writers, commencing with the earliest
account of Irish history, and carried down to the
year of our Lord, 1750, with a descriptive catalogue
of such of their works as are still extant in verse or
prose, consisting of upwards of one thousand sepa-

rate tracts." This valuable book, which has been
long out of print, is the only attempt ever made at
a complete list of Irish Gaelic writers. It is of course
exceedingly defective, but yet a wonderful compilation for O'Reilly to have accomplished single-handed,
considering the way in which Irish manuscripts were
at that time dispersed in private hands, or stored in
inaccessible libraries, unarranged and uncatalogued.
I do not think it would be difficult for a worker in
the same field at the present day to double the number of writers named by O'Reilly. Unfortunately, of
what is perhaps the most valuable part of our literature, our anonymous epics, ballads, and romances,
he gives no account whatsoever. A full history of our
Irish writers, conducted on O'Reilly's method, would
be a book of national importance, but since the death
of O'Curry Ireland has, I fear, seen no man equally
qualified to undertake it.

This great scholar himself was the third and last
person to attempt something like a chronological
survey of early Irish literature. He devotes no less
than 130 pages of his *Manners and Customs* to the

history of *Education and Literature in Ancient Erinn*, mentioning the most important poets from the earliest times to the eleventh century.

The present slight attempt to sketch the story of our native literature carries us down to about the close of the Danish invasions. The Middle and Modern Irish period, with the history of the Bardic schools, the story of the development of our poetry, an explanation of our system of metric, and an account of the more modern romances, would require a volume or two volumes to themselves.

In conclusion, I have to thank my friends, Father Eugene O'Growney and Mr. David Comyn, the former for so kindly placing at my disposal his unpublished lectures on Early Irish Christian Literature, and the latter for the loan of rare books and valuable MSS., and much other kind assistance.

CONTENTS.

THE STORY OF
EARLY GAELIC LITERATURE.

CHAPTER I.

EARLY USE OF LETTERS AMONG THE IRISH.

HE first question which confronts us in our sketch of Irish literature is: When did we begin to have an Irish literature? The answer is difficult; it depends upon that other question: When did the Irish begin to use an alphabet and to write? The existing alphabet, which has been used from the time of St. Patrick at least, is only a modification of the Roman one, and it may fairly be surmised that the *general* introduction of it into

B

Ireland is due to Christian missionaries. There is no reason, however, for supposing that it was St. Patrick or any other saint who introduced it. There must have been many isolated persons in Ireland in the fourth century, if not before, who were acquainted with the Roman letters. St. Chrysostom, in his "Demonstration that Christ is God," written in the year 387, mentions that already churches and altars had been erected in the British Islands, and St.-Jerome, in his Commentary on the Epistle to the Ephesians, written about 392, abuses in his usual slashing style the Irishman, Celestius, who had been criticizing some of that Saint's writings. "Stolidissimus," he calls him, "et Scotorum pultibus prægravatus," which freely translated means that he was "a great omadhaun, and had his wits as heavy as his paunch from eating Irish stirabout." Gennadius,* however, writing about one hundred years later, mentions that this same Irishman, Celestius, while still a youth, wrote three epistles in the form of little books, to his parents, who must, I suppose, in fairness be assumed to have been able to read them. Already, from the beginning of the third century at the least, says Zimmer in his *Keltische Studien*, British missionaries were at work in the south of Ireland. The account in the *Acta Sanctorum* of Declan Bishop of Waterford, said to have been born in 347, and of Ailbe, another southern bishop who met St. Patrick, is looked upon by Zimmer as perfectly true so far as it relates to the actual existence of these pre-Patrician bishops; and Bede, in his history, distinctly says that Palladius was sent from

---

* See the preface to O'Donovan's Grammar, but I have been unable to verify the quotation.

Rome, *ad Scottos in Christum credentes*—"to the Irish who believed in Christ."

But it may be objected, Ireland had the Ogam * alphabet, and may have produced a previous literature written in it. This is indeed a very important but an immensely difficult question. Monsieur d'Arbois de Jubainville, who has studied our literary antiquities to greater purpose than perhaps anyone else, seems inclined to believe in the antiquity of this alphabet. Discussing the story of St. Patrick's setting a Latin

* I have often heard this word pronounced of late as Oggam, which is certainly wrong. In later times the "g" often became "aspirated," and was not pronounced. The Munstermen pronounced the word as if written úgham (*i.e.*, oom, rhyming with room); in Connacht it would have been most likely pronounced "ome," rhyming to home, but the best pronunciation of it in either Irish or English is to leave the "g" unaspirated, and pronounce it as if rhyming to *rogue 'em*, or *póg 'am*.

This alphabet, as everyone knows, consisted of a number of short lines, straight or slanting, drawn through over or under, one long line. Thus, four short straight cuts or lines to the right of or below the long line stand for S, above they mean C; passing through the long line, half on one side and half on the other, they mean E. These straight lines being easily cut with a chisel on stone, continued long in use. They do not seem to have been common to the whole "Irish" race, but to some southern branch of it, for out of about 170 Ogam inscriptions not more than a score are found outside Kerry, Cork, and Waterford. Yet there is no trace in our literature of the power of writing Ogams having been a special peculiarity of any sect or of any place, and they are in our literature as freely attributed to Ulster, where none are found, as to Munster, where they abound. Many have been translated with comparative ease, and their language seems like that of the Gaulish inscriptions, *Maqi* as the genitive of Mac, etc. Others again seem to defy translation, and all kinds of attempts have been made to unriddle them, treating them as though they were written in cypher. We have also several specimens of Ogams cut on small articles, such as gold or leaden ornaments, sufficient to show that their use was by no means confined to pillar or grave stones.

alphabet before Fiach the day he was consecrated, and of Fiach's being able to read Psalms within the following four-and-twenty hours, he remarks that the story is just possible, since Fiach should have known the Ogam alphabet, and except for the form of the letters it and the Latin alphabet were the same. Others, however, have asserted that the Ogam alphabet is not an alphabet at all, but is only a cryptic post-Christian way of writing the Latin letters. One thing is certain, that the Ogam alphabet continued in use for inscriptions on pillar and tombstones until a comparatively late period, probably until the Danish invasions were over. Even supposing this alphabet to have been indigenous and pre-Christian, still, though it may have been used by the ollavs and poets to perpetuate tribe names and genealogies, it must have been too rude a contrivance to produce anything like a flourishing literature. It is, however, as far as we know, only with the coming of Patrick * that Ire-

---

* The Confession and Epistle attributed to St. Patrick, and partly found in the *Book of Armagh,* a codex dating from the year 812, are by Whitley Stokes and many other writers admitted as genuine. Giraldus Cambrensis, too, speaks of (*Top. Hib.,* ch. 33) " Patrick and Columkille, whose books, written in Irish, are still extant amongst them," *i.e.,* the Irish. The term used by Giraldus, however, *Hibernicé scripti,* may perhaps mean written in Irish characters. Yet Patrick himself appears to say that he originally wrote in Irish, "*sermo et loquela mea translata est in linquam alienam sicut facile potest probari ex saliva scripturæ meæ,*" *i.e.,* " My words and language have been translated into another tongue, as may easily be judged from my beslavered writing." There has, however, been an attack lately made upon the genuineness of St. Patrick's writings in an article by J. V. Pflugk-Harttung in the *Neues Heidelberger Jahrbuch,* Jahrgang III., Heft I., 1893, in which he tries to prove by internal evidence that both Confession and Epistle, especially the former, are somewhat later than St.

land may be said to have become, properly speaking, a literary country. The churches and monasteries established by him soon became so many nuclei of learning, and from the end of the fifth century a knowledge of letters had completely permeated the island. So suddenly does this appear to have taken place, and so rapidly does Ireland seem to have produced a flourishing literature of laws, poems, and sagas, that it is difficult or impossible not to believe that our people had before this arrived at a very high state of indigenous culture. " I assert," says Dr. Sigerson, speaking of the laws at the revision of which St. Patrick is said to have assisted, " that, speaking biologically, such laws could not emanate from any race whose brains had not been subject to the quickening influences of education for many generations." But indeed it is pretty certain that even the pre-Christian Irish were not by any means uncultured. Already in the first century Tacitus could write of our island that its ports and harbours were well known through merchants and commerce.* Its earliest saga literature, too, is absolutely Pagan both in subject and tone, leading one very much to wonder how the abundance of heathen incidents with which it abounds could have been preserved had the pre-Christian bards possessed

Patrick's time. Yet he, too, seems to believe in the antiquity of the Irish Ogam characters. St. Patrick mentions that after his flight from Ireland he saw a man coming as it were from that country with innumerable letters to him, whereupon the critic remarks that it is hard to understand how Patrick came by the idea that a man could bring him " innumerable letters from the heathen Ireland of that time, where, except for Ogams and inscribed stones *(ausser Oghams und Skulpturzeichen)*, the art of writing was yet unknown." This is going much too far.

* *Agricola*, ch. 24.

no other than oral methods of transmitting their knowledge. We must remember, too, that several of the
old Irish romances which relate to exclusively Pagan
times and Pagan transactions, and which were probably existing in very nearly their present forms as
early as the seventh century, refer to Ogam writing,
and such written messages as could not have been
conveyed by mere picture signs, but to missives of
more intricate import.*

While the present Irish names for books, reading,
writing, letters, pens, and parchment† are certainly
derived from the Latin, it appears that there were
also older words in use designating the ancient writing
materials of the Gael. Thus the Dialogue of the
Sages records how Diarmuid mac Fergus *Cerrbhebil*

---

* See O'Curry's *MS. Mat.*, p. 463, where he has collected the
earliest account of Pagan writing from our oldest MSS.

Thus we find in the *Book of Leinster* a story about Corc,
son of a Pagan King of Munster, who was exiled by his father.
He fled to Scotland, to the Court of King Feradach, and not
knowing how the king might receive him, hid in a wood
near by. The king's poet, however, met and recognised him,
having seen him before that in Ireland ; and noticed an Ogam
written on the prince's shield. "Who was it that befriended
you with that Ogam," asked the poet, "for it was not good luck
which he designed for you?" "Why," asked the prince, "what
does it contain?" "What it contains," said the poet, "is this :
that if by day you arrive at the Court of Feradach the King, your
head shall be struck off before night ; if it be at night you arrive,
that your head shall be struck off before morning." The classical
scholar need hardly be reminded of the striking resemblance
between this and the σήματα λυγρὰ, which, according to
Homer, Prœtus gave the· unsuspecting Bellerophon to bring to
the King of Lycia :

γράψας ἐν πίνακι πτυκτῷ θυμοφθόρα πολλά.

† Leabhar, léigheadh, scríobhadh, litreacha, peann, meam-
ram.

orders the words of *Caoilte* and Ossian to be inscribed on *Tamhlorgaibh fileadh,* or "the headless-staffs" (as O'Curry translates it) "of poets," and it was done accordingly. The poets appear in most ancient times to have carried square staffs, upon the lines and angles of which they wrote, or rather cut or scratched with a knife in the Birch-Alder alphabet, or in other words in Ogam characters, and if, as O'Curry has surmised, the "tablet-staff" of the poet was really of the nature of a fan which could close up in the shape of a square stick, we may well imagine the almost superstitious reverence which in rude times must have attached itself, and which as we know did attach itself to the man who could carry about in his hand the whole history and genealogy of his race, and probably the catch-words of innumerable poems and the skeletons of highly-prized narratives.

Amongst the many accounts of pre-Christian writing there is one so curious that I shall give it *in extenso.**

The Story of Baile Mac Buain, the Sweet Spoken.

"Buain's only son was Baile.† He was specially beloved by Aillinn,‡ the daughter of Lewy Farriga, —but some say she was the daughter of Owen, son of Dathi—and he was specially beloved not of her only, but of every one who ever heard or saw him, on account of his delightful stories.

"Now Baile and Aillinn made an appointment to

---

* O'Curry found this piece in the MS. marked II. 3. 18. in Trinity College, Dublin, and has printed it at page 472 of his *Manuscript Materials.*
† Pronounced Balla or Bolla.
‡ Pronounced Al-yinn.

meet at Rosnaree, on the banks of the Boyne in Bregia. And he came from Emania, in the north, to meet her, passing over Slieve Fuad and *Muirtheimhne* to *Tráigh mBaile* [Dundalk], and here he and his troops unyoked their chariots, sent their horses out to pasture, and gave themselves up to pleasure and happiness.

"And while they were there they saw a horrible spectral personage coming towards them from the south. Vehement was his step and his rapid progress. The way he sped over the earth might be compared to the darting of a hawk down a cliff or to wind from off the green sea, and his left was towards the land [*i.e.*, he came from the south along the shore].

"'Go meet him,' said Baile, 'and ask him where he goes, or whence he comes, or what is the cause of his haste.'

"'From Mount Leinster I come, and I go back now to the north, to the mouth of the River Bann ; and I have no news but of the daughter of Lewy, son of Fergus, who had fallen in love with Baile mac Buain, and was coming to meet him. But the youths of Leinster overtook her, and she died from being forcibly detained, as Druids and fair prophets had prophecied, for they foretold that they would never meet in life, but that they would meet after death and not part for ever. There is my news.' And he darted away from them like a blast of wind over the green sea, and they were not able to detain him.

"When Baile heard this he fell dead without life, and his tomb and his rath were raised, and his stone set up, and his funeral games* were performed by the Ultonians.

* Literally, " Fair of Lamentation."

"And a yew grew up through his grave, and the form and shape of Baile's head was visible on the top of it. — Whence the place is called Baile's Strand [now Dundalk].

"Afterwards the same man went to the south to where the maiden Aillinn was, and went into her greeanaun or sunny chamber.

"'Whence comes the man whom we do not know?' said the maiden.

"'From the northern half of Erin, from the mouth of the Bann I come, and I go past this to Mount Leinster.'

"'You have news?' said the maiden.

"'I have no news worth mentioning now, only I saw the Ultonians performing the funeral games and digging the rath, and setting up the stone, and writing the name of Baile mac Buain, the royal heir of Ulster, by the side of the Strand of Baile, who died while on his way to meet a sweetheart and a beloved woman to whom he had given affection, for it was not fated for them to meet in life, or for one of them to see the other living.' And he darted out after telling the evil news.

"And Aillinn fell dead, without life, and her tomb was raised, etc. And an apple tree grew through her grave and became a great tree at the end of seven years, and the shape of Aillinn's head was upon its top.

"Now at the end of seven years, poets and prophets and visioners cut down the yew which was over the grave of Baile, and they made a poet's tablet of it, and they wrote the visions and the espousals and the loves and the courtships of Ulster in it. [The apple tree which grew over the grave of Aillinn was also cut down] and in like manner the courtships of Leinster were written in it.

"There came a November Eve long afterwards, and a festival was made to celebrate it by Art, the son of Conn [of the Hundred Battles, High King of Ireland] and the professors of every science came to that feast, as was their custom, and they brought their tablets with them. And these tablets also came there, and Art saw them, and when he saw them he asked for them; and the two tablets were brought, and he held them in his hands face to face. Suddenly the one tablet of them sprang upon the other, and they became united the same as a woodbine round a twig,* and it was not possible to separate them. And they were preserved like every other jewel in the treasury at Tara, until it was burned by Dúnlang, son of Enna, at the time that he burnt the princesses at Tara, as has been said,

> The apple tree of noble Aillinn
> The yew of Baile—small inheritance—
> Though they are introduced into poems
> Unlearned people do not understand them.

And Ailbhè, daughter of Cormac, grandson of Conn [of the Hundred Battles] said too,

> What I liken Lumluine to
> Is to the yew of Baile's rath,
> What I liken the other to
> Is to the apple-tree of Aillinn."

So far this strange tale. But poetic as it is, it yields —unlike most—its chief value when rationalized, for as O'Curry remarks it was evidently invented to

---

* See a similar story about two trees at page 59 of my *Love Songs of Connacht.*

account for some inscribed tablets in the reign of King Art in the second century, which had—as we ourselves have seen is the case with so many leaves of very old manuscripts at this day—become fastened to each other, so that they clung inextricably together and could not be separated.

Now the massacre of the princesses at Tara happened according to the Four Masters in the year 241, when the tablets were burnt. Hence, one of two things must be the case ; the story must either have originated *before* that date to account for the sticking together of the tablets, or else some one must have invented it long afterwards, that is, must, without any apparent cause, have invented a story out of his own head, as to how there were *once on a time* two tablets made of trees which *once* grew on two tombs, which were *once* fastened together before Art, son of Conn, and which were soon afterwards unfortunately burnt—a supposition, which, considering there were then, *ex hypothesis*, no adhering tablets to prompt the invention, appears to be in the highest degree improbable.

CHAPTER II.

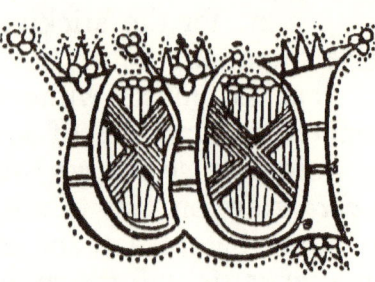ITH the establishment of Christianity, Latin literature began to be studied and Latin to be written in Ireland. It never superseded Irish, however, as either an epistolary or literary medium, but the native language was no doubt cultivated all the better from having Latin used to some small extent, side by side with it.

Books now began to be multiplied in Ireland, and the trade of a scribe seems to have been a highly honourable one. The Venerable Bede, himself an Anglo-Saxon, tells us * how a multitude of his countrymen, both nobles and common people, fled out of England into Ireland during a time of plague, about the year 664, and were warmly welcomed by the Gaels, who took care that they should be provided with food every day, without payment, and that they should have books to read, and also that they should receive gratuitous instruction from

* Bede, *Hist.*, iii., 27.

Irish masters. Books, then, must have already multiplied considerably when a host of hungry Anglo-Saxons could thus be supplied with them, and with gratuitous instruction as well, just as almost down to our own day,—down in fact to the establishment of our un-national national schools,—in pursuance of this noble and truly Irish tradition, "poor scholars" were freely supported by the people and helped in their studies.

Columbanus, born in Leinster, A.D. 543, who evangelized a great part of Burgundy and Switzerland, and who was educated at the Monastery of Bangor, on Belfast Lough, was as cultured a Latin scholar and poet as could be met with in any part of Europe outside of Italy.* His Latin verses are marvellous for his age and time. Irish monasteries and seats of learning seem to have been sought out by vast numbers of foreigners from the sixth to the ninth century.

Indeed, it has always appeared to me that, despite its insular position, Ireland has during the course of its history been as little insular and as little insulated in the ethical sense of the word as any country in the world. At one time our people were in close connection with Scandinavia and the north of Europe, at another were close friends of the Spaniards, at another scarcely a noble family in the kingdom who had not one of its members in France, and now there is hardly a family, rich or poor, which has not a friend or relative in the New World to enlarge its mind and keep it

---

* "It is sufficient," says Jubainville, "to glance at the writings of Columbanus to immediately recognize his marvellous superiority over Gregory of Tours and the Gallo-Romans of his time. He lived in close converse with the classical authors, as later on did the learned men of the 16th century, whose equal he certainly is not, but of whom he seems a sort of precursor."

in touch with wider sympathies. And at this early
period during the sixth, seventh, eighth and ninth
centuries, there appears to have been a close and constant connection in the way of trade, learning, and
emigration between Ireland and the south of Gaul.
We find Gaulish merchants at Clonmacnois on the
Shannon, in the centre of Ireland, selling wine to St.
Ciaran (Kieran), in the middle of the sixth century.
We find Columbanus enquiring at Nantes for a vessel
engaged in the Irish trade. Adamnan's treatise on
Holy Places was written from an account of them
given him by a Gaul who had travelled. Gaulish
sailors bring Columkille news of an Italian city
burned down. In the old Irish poem on the Fair
of Carman, a Pagan institution which survived far
into Christian times, we find mention of the

"Great market of the foreign Greeks,
   Where gold and noble clothes were wont to be" *

—the foreign Greeks being doubtless the Greek-
speaking Gaulish merchants. In Ward's *Life of St.
Rumdel*, he quotes from the Litany of Aengus the
Culdee, a work at that time seven or eight hundred
years old, in which mention is made of the great
number of foreigners who found their way by sea to
Ireland between the years 500 and 800, including
Gauls, Saxons, Britons, Romans, Latins, and seven
Egyptian monks. In the days of St. Cuthaldus,
about the year 700, Gauls, Teutons, Swiss, and
Italians are found crowding to Lismore,† and there

---

* Margadh mór na n Gall n Greugach
   I m bíonn ór a's áird-eudach.
† Ussher, *Antiquities*, Works, VI., 303, quoted by Professor
Stokes in *Proceedings of the R.I. Academy*, May, 1892, p. 191,
in an interesting article chiefly based upon Sullivan.

appears during these centuries to have been a brisk
and increasing intercourse kept up between Ireland
and Gaul, not through England, but by an independent sea route.

It was, of course, the fame of our native schools
which induced such crowds of scholars to visit them,
and the instruction imparted in the monasteries—
which seem to have been almost as much secular
colleges as ecclesiastical institutions—comprehended
a wide range of study, perfectly wonderful considering
how the darkness of the Middle Ages had already
set in over the struggles, agony and confusion of feudal
Europe. Greek, which had all but died out as a
liberal study elsewhere, was taught in Ireland.
Hebrew seems to have been studied in some univer-
sities. Virgil, Ovid, Terence, and most of the Latin
poets, were of course widely read. The art of Latin
verse must have been well taught, and it may easily be
supposed other studies such as arithmetic, grammar,
chronology, etc., were more than kept up to the level
of the times. Columbanus discusses points of Hebrew
scholarship, and Archbishop Ussher tells us that he
himself saw the Psalter of St. Camin of Inis Caltra in
Lough Derg, "having a collection of the Hebrew
text placed on the upper part of each page, and with
brief scholia added on the outside margin;" while
we have still extant a letter of St. Cummian of Durrow,
in the King's County, written in the year 634 to the
Abbot of I-Columkille, or Iona, on which Professor
Stokes thus comments: "I call it a marvellous composition because of the vastness of its learning. It
quotes, besides the Scriptures and Latin authors,
Greek writers like Origen, Cyril, Pachomius the
head and reformer of Egyptian monasticism, and
Damascius, the last of the celebrated Neo-Platonic

philosophers of Athens, who lived about the year
500, and wrote all his works in Greek.   Cummian
discusses the calendars of the Macedonians, Hebrews,
and Copts, giving us the Hebrew, Greek, and Egyptian names of months and cycles, and tells us that
he had been sent as one of a deputation of learned
men a few years before to ascertain the practice of the
Church of Rome [with regard to Easter].   When they
came to Rome they lodged in one hostelry with a
Greek and a Hebrew, an Egyptian and a Scythian,
who told them that the whole world celebrated the
Roman and not the Irish Easter."   This long letter,
remarks Stokes, proves the fact to demonstration that
in the first half of the seventh century there was a wide
range of Greek learning, not ecclesiastical merely,
but chronological, astronomical, and philosophical,
away at Durrow, in the very centre of the Bog of
Allen.   It also shows the eagerness with which the
learned Irish of that day strove to be abreast of
everything that was to be known, and the pains
they took not to remain in ignorance.

But was all this instruction thus imparted in the
many monasteries and schools of Ireland, conveyed to
the foreign students through the medium of the Irish
language?   It would appear so, for the very oldest
codices of gospels and other Latin books, preserved in
the libraries on the continent, are full of glosses and
words in Irish written on the margin or between the
lines, and it is these scanty remnants of eighth and
ninth century Irish which now go under the name of
Old Irish to distinguish it from the Middle Irish in
which most of our old literature is written ; and it is
these glosses which give the oldest form of the
language, and which, upon examination, proved of
such value, that in the hands of the great philologist

Zeuss, they once and for all established the fact that the Irish, like the Greeks, Teutons, and Sclavs, belonged to the Aryan race, or rather spoke a pure Aryan language. It is highly probable that all the students who flocked to Durrow, Lismore, Bangor, and the other Irish schools, learned the language of the country, and possibly many of them found themselves as much attracted by the lore of the bards as by the learning of the ecclesiastics. Few incomers could have remained uninfluenced by bardic teaching in a country where the man of song and his colleges ranked almost as high in popular regard as the professor of theology and his monastic institutions. We know of at least one celebrated pupil who fell under their influence, Aldfred, King of the Northumbrian Saxons, who passed, as Bede tells us, his time in study while in Ireland, and when leaving it wrote a poem of 60 lines* in the Irish language and metre which he must have learned from the bards, upon what he had found there. Mangan made the following translation of it for Montgomery more literally than was his wont:—

ALDFRED'S ITINERARY.

" I found in Innisfail the fair,
In Ireland, while in exile there,
Women of worth, both grave and gay men,
Many clerics and many laymen.

* O'Reilly states that it contained 96 lines, but I think this is erroneous. Hardiman had a vellum copy of it, in which he said the "character was ancient and very obscure." Aldfred was called Fiann Fionn by the Irish, and his mother was of Irish descent. If this be really his poem, only modified in course of transcription,—and it may very well be his,—the intention seems to have been to pay for the hospitality he had received with a song to the whole nation.

C

" I travelled its fruitful provinces round,
  And in every one of the five I found—
  Alike in church and in palace hall—
  Abundant apparel and food for all.

" Gold and silver I found, and money,
  Plenty of wheat and plenty of honey.
  I found God's people rich in pity ;
  Found many a feast and many a city.

" I also found in Armagh the splendid,
  Meekness, wisdom, and prudence blended :
  Fasting as Christ hath recommended,
  And noble councillors untranscended.

" I found in each great church moreo'er,
  Whether on island or on shore,
  Piety, learning, fond affection ;
  Holy welcome and kind protection.

" I found the good lay monks and brothers
  Ever beseeching help for others,
  And in their keeping the holy word,
  Pure as it came from JESUS the LORD.

" I found in Munster, unfettered of any,
  Kings and queens and poets a many.
  Poets well-skilled in music and measure ;
  Prosperous doings, mirth and pleasure.

" I found in Connacht the just, redundance
  Of riches, milk in lavish abundance ;
  Hospitality, vigour, fame,
  In Cruachan's land of heroic name.

　　　　*　　*　　*　　*　　*

" I found in Ulster, from hill to glen,
  Hardy warriors, resolute men.
  Beauty that bloomed when youth was gone,
  And strength transmitted from sire to son.

　　　*　　　*　　*　　*　　*

" I found in Leinster the smooth and sleek,
From Dublin to Slewmargy's peak,
Flourishing pastures, valour, health,
Song-loving worthies, commerce, wealth.

" I found besides from Ara to Glea
In the broad rich country of Ossory,
Sweet fruits, good laws, for all and each,
Great chess-players, men of truthful speech.

" I found in Meath's fair principality,
Virtue, vigour, and hospitality ;
Candour, joyfulness, bravery, purity—
Ireland's bulwark and security.

" I found strict morals in age and youth,
I found historians recording truth.
The things I sing of in verse unsmooth
I found them all—I have written sooth."

We have now seen to what a pitch classical learning
arrived during the centuries which followed the introduction of Christianity. How far was native literature
cultivated ?

Before attempting to answer this question we must
bear in mind two things ; first, the wholesale destruction of our native documents by the Danes and the
English ; secondly, the practise of altering the orthography and even the words of old writers when the
language they employed was becoming obsolete. The
first of these things has so destroyed our literary
records that we can now only guess at what they once
were ; the second has rendered it nearly impossible
to tell whether a poem ascribed to a bard of the fourth
or fifth century, but itself written in the language of the

eleventh or twelfth or some still later century, is really
the work—modernized up to date—of the poet whose
composition it professes to be.

We must first glance at the list of lost books drawn
up by O'Curry, which may be supposed to have contained our earliest literature. We find the poet Senchan
Torpéist, according to an account in a twelfth century
manuscript, the *Book of Leinster*, complaining that the
only perfect record of the great Táin Bo Chuailgne or
Cattle-spoil of Cooley, had been taken to the East with
the *Cuilmenn* or great Skin Book. Now, Zimmer, who
made a special study of this story, and those best qualified to judge, consider that the earliest redaction of
the great Táin Bo story dates from the seventh century.
This legend about Senchan (a real historical poet
whose poems in praise of Columkille we still possess)
is probably equally old, and points to the early existence of a great skin book in which Pagan tales were
written, and which was then lost. This, of course, is
rather shadowy, but the next lost book is alluded to
in a no doubt genuine poem by Cuan O'Lochain,
about the year 1000, in which he says that Cormac
mac Airt drew up the Saltair of Tara. Cormac being
a Pagan, could not have called his compilation a Saltair
or Psalterium, but it may have got the name afterwards. All that this really proves is that in the year
1000, there existed a book about the prerogatives of
Tara and the provincial kings, so old that the poet
Cuan O'Lochain was not afraid to ascribe it—no doubt
following tradition—to Cormac mac Airt, of the second
century. The next lost book is the Book of the Uacong-
bhail, upon which both the O'Clerys in their Book
of Invasions and Keating in his History, drew, and
which, according to O'Curry, still existed at Kildare as
late as 1626. The next book is called the Cin of Drom

Snechta.   It is quoted in the Leabhar na h-Uidhre,*
or Book of the Dun Cow, a MS. of about the year
1100, and often in the *Book of Ballymote*, and by
Keating, who, in quoting it, says, "And it was before
the coming of Patrick to Ireland that that book
existed;" while the *Book of Leinster*, compiled in the
middle of the twelfth century, has this note: "[Ernin
son of] Duach, son of the King of Connacht, an
ollav and a prophet, and a professor in history, and
a professor in wisdom, it was he that collected the
genealogies and histories of the men of Erin into one
book, that is the Cin Droma Snechta." Now, there are
only two Duachs mentioned amongst the Kings of Connacht, one a Pagan, grandson of Eochaidh Muighm-
hedhoin (Mwee-vé-on) who died A.D. 379, and the
other, who died, according to the Four Masters, in 499.
In Keating's time the tradition evidently was that the
earlier of these was father of the author of the book.
Whichever it be, it still points to a high early civiliza-
tion. The only other supposition is that the writer of the
twelfth century note in the *Book of Leinster* deliberately
ascribed the then existing book—whose pedigree must
have been pretty well known—to someone who never
wrote it at all.   This is possible; is it probable?   It
is only probable on the supposition that the tenth and
twelfth century writers entered into a tacit conspiracy
to ascribe their books and records to the earliest source
possible, in order to increase their value.   But as we
know that there were almost certainly books in Ireland
in St. Patrick's time, it seems highly unreasonable to
deliberately put down the statement in the *Book of*

---

* Pronounced L'yowr (rhyming with "hour") na Heera.
hUidhre is the genitive feminine of *odhar*, dun-coloured, and the
word *bo*, a cow, is understood.

Leinster as a conscious invention, and the tradition of Keating as worthless and of no weight. The next books we find an account of, were said to have belonged to St. Longarad, a contemporary of Columkille. The scribe who wrote the glosses to the *Festology* of Aengus the Culdee, said that these books existed still, but that no man could read them, which he accounts for by the tale that Columkille once paid Longarad a visit in order to see his books, but that his host refused to show them to him, and that then Columkille said, "May your books be of no use after you, since you have shown inhospitality about them." On account of this the books became illegible after Longarad's death. Aengus the Culdee lived about the year 800, though Stokes thinks that the *Festology*, or Calendar of Saints, which passes under his name, could not have been composed much before the end of the tenth century. It is uncertain when the Scholiast wrote his note about these books, but it also is very old. It is plain, then, that at this time a number of illegible books, illegible no doubt from age, existed ; and to account for this illegibility the story of Columkille's curse was invented. The *Annals of Ulster* quote another book at the year 527, under the name of the Book of St. Mochta, who was a disciple of St. Patrick. They also quote the Book of Cuana, at the year 468, and repeatedly afterwards down to the year 610, while they record the death of Cuana, a scribe, at the year 738, after which no more quotations from Cuana's book occur. The following books, almost all of which existed before the year 1100, are also, according to O'Curry, alluded to in our old literature :—The Book of Dubhdaleithe ; the Yellow Book of Slane ; the original Leabhar na h-Uidhre ; the Books of Eochaidh O'Flannagain ; a certain book known as the book eaten by the poor people in the desert; the Book of Inis an Duin; the short Book of Monasterboice; the Books of Flann of Monasterboice; the Book of Flann of Dungiven; the Book of Downpatrick; the Book of Derry; the Book of *Sábhal Phátraic;* the Black Book of St. Molaga; the Yellow Book of St. Moling; the Yellow Book of Mac Murrough; the Book of Armagh (not that now so called); the Red Book of Mac Egan; the Speckled Book of Mac Egan; the Long Book of Leithlin; the Books of O'Scoba of Clonmacnois; the *Duil* of Drom Ceat; the Book of Clonsost; the Book of Cluain Eidhneach in Leix; and one of the most valuable and often quoted of all, Cormac's great Saltair of Cashel,* compiled by Cormac mac Cullinan, who

---

* " At what time this book was lost," says O'Curry, " we have no precise knowledge, but that it existed, though in a dilapidated state in the year 1454, is evident from the fact that there is in the Bodleian Library in Oxford (Laud, 610) a copy of such portions of it as could be deciphered at that time, made by Shawn O'Clery for Mac Rickard Butler. From the contents of this copy, and from the frequent references to the original for history and genealogies found in the Books of Ballymote, Lecan, and others, it must have been an historical and genealogical compilation of large size and great diversity." A legible copy of the Saltair appears, however, to have existed at a much later date. I discovered a curious poem in an uncatalogued MS. in the Royal Irish Academy, by one David Condon, written probably about the year 1680, some time between the Cromwellian and Williamite wars, in which he says :—

Salcaiṗ Chaiṗill iṗ ᴅeaṗḃh ᵹuṗ léiᵹheaᵹ·ᵹa
leaḃaṗ Ṡhleanna·ᴅá·locha ᵹan ᵹó ḃa léiᵹ ᴅaṁ,
leaḃaṗ Ḃuiᴅhe ṁuiᵹhleann(?) oḃaiṗ aoṗᴅa, etc.,

i.e., "Surely I have read the Saltair of Cashel, and the Book of Glendalough was certainly plain to me, and the Yellow Book of Muighleann (=Moling?), an ancient work, the Book of Molaga, and the Lessons of Cionnfaola . . . and many more (books) along with them which are not (now) found in Ireland." For this interesting poem see my forthcoming *Báird agus Bárduigheacht.*

was at once King of Munster and Archbishop of Cashel, and who fell in battle in 903, according to the chronology of the Four Masters. These are probably only a very few indeed, of the books in which our enormous early literature was contained, but which have now perished almost to a page.

Where, then, may a few small and scanty branches of what was once a mighty earth-shadowing tree be still picked up? The two MSS. of by far the most importance in the way of miscellaneous literature, are the Leabhar na h-Uidhre and the Book of Leinster, transcribed about the year 1100 and 1150 respectively, and after them the most important of our surviving great parchment books, are the Book of Ballymote, the Leabhar Breac, or Speckled Book, and the Book of Lecan. After them, and of nearly equal importance come a number of vellum books preserved in Trinity College, Dublin, the British Museum, and the Bodleian at Oxford.

CHAPTER III.

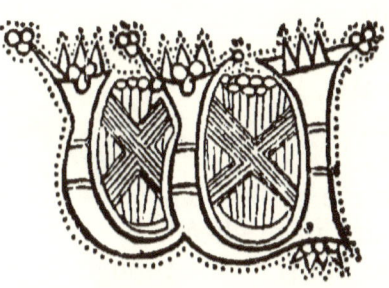E must now take a look at the poetry ascribed in our oldest manuscripts to poets who lived either before our era, or during the first six or eight centuries, and at the more scanty prose remains of our early native literature. The first poem written in Ireland is said to have been the work of Amergin, who was brother of Evir, Ir and Eremon, the first Milesian princes who colonized Ireland many hundreds of years before Christ. The three short pieces of verse ascribed to Amergin are certainly very ancient and very strange. But, as the whole story of the Milesian invasion is wrapped in mystery and is quite possibly only a rationalized account of early Irish mythology (in which the Tuatha De Danann, Firbolgs, and possibly Milesians, are nothing but the gods of the early Irish euhemerized into men) no faith can be placed in the alleged date or genuineness of Amergin's verses. They are, however, of interest, because as Irish tradition has always represented them as being the first

verses made in Ireland, so it may very well be that they actually do present the oldest surviving lines in any vernacular tongue in Europe except Greek.

The following is noticeable for its curious pantheistic strain which reminds one strangely of the East :—

> I am the wind which breathes upon the sea,
> I am the wave of the ocean,
> I am the murmur of the billows,
> I am the ox of the seven combats,
> I am the vulture upon the rock,
> I am a beam of the sun,
> I am the fairest of plants,
> I am a wild boar in valour,
> I am a salmon in the water,
> I am a lake in the plain,
> I am a word of science,
> I am the point of the lance of battle,
> I am the God who creates in the head.
>   [*i.e.*, of man] the fire [*i.e.*, the thought].
> Who is it who throws light into the meeting on the
>   mountain ?
> Who announces the ages of the moon [If not I] ?
> Who teaches the place where couches the sun [If
>   not I] ?

The laws said to have been written by Ollamh Fodhla six or seven centuries before Christ, and those fragments ascribed to Cimbaeth three centuries later, may be passed over. Even the annalist Tighernach, in the tenth century has said *omnia ante Cimbaeth incerta sunt* * or, "all things up to the time of Cimbaeth

* Why Tighearnach chose a comparatively unimportant name like Cimbaeth as the starting point of true history is mysterious enough, for he was not the founder of a dynasty, or as far as we know particularly remarkable in any way.

are uncertain." But, what shall we say of the poems ascribed to Feirceirtne *file*, accredited author of *Uiricept na nEigeas*, his rival Neide, Athairne the Satirist, Congal, son of Eochaidh Feidhlioch (Yohee Failyuch), Lughar the poet of Méve Queen of Connacht, all of whom lived according to our accounts before, but not long before, the time of Christ's birth. What are we to say further to the poems ascribed to King Art the Solitary, Finn mac Cool,* Ossian and *Caoilte* (Cweelt-yă) in the third century, to the pieces in prose and verse of Cormac mac Art, monarch of Ireland, and Olioll Olum of the same period? What shall we say of the poems ascribed to Dubhthach (Duv-hach) O'Lugair, or of Torna Eigeas in the fifth century? All that can be laid down with certainty is that the poems ascribed to these writers as we find them in codices of the twelfth and later centuries, are for the most part couched in language too modern to have been possibly used by the supposed authors. In others again, internal evidence would appear to show that they can hardly have been in their entirety the work of the authors to whom they have been ascribed,† while

---

* Such names as Finn mac Cool, Ossian (in Irish Oisín, pronounced Essheen), Méve (in Irish Méddh, often curiously pronounced " Mou " in Connacht), Lewy (in Irish Lughaidh), and a few more, have become so adopted into English that I have let them stand. The Mac of these pre-Christian names should best be spelt with a small m to show that it is not part of a surname, but really means "son of." The name Art when preceded by Mac becomes Airt in Irish, but I have not inflected it for fear of confusing the English reader.

† As in the poem in the *Book of Leinster* ascribed to O'Lugair, circiter 430, printed by O'Curry, *MS. Mat.*, p. 493, where the poet speaking of Enna Censelach's campaigns, says that they unyoked their steeds upon the rampart of " Casil Cliaraig," Clerical Cashel.

again, there are some in which the language seems
more ancient and the spirit purely Pagan. Of
most of them, however, it may safely be asserted that
their language, if the work of the supposed writers, has
been very much modified before it came down to us.

This modification of language is not uncommon in
literature, and takes place naturally; but I doubt if
there ever was a literature in which it played the same
important part as in ours. Thus, let us take the story
of the Táin Bo Chuailgne, of which I shall have more
to say later on. The German philologist, Zimmer,
after long and careful study of the text as presented to
us in a manuscript of about the year 1100, came to
the conclusion, from the marks of old Irish inflexion
and so forth, which still remain in the eleventh century
text, that there had been two recensions of the story,
a pre-Danish—that is, a seventh or eighth century one,
and a post-Danish—that is, a tenth or eleventh century
one. Thus, the epic may have been originally committed to paper in the seventh century, modified in
the tenth, transcribed into the manuscripts in which
we have it in the eleventh and twelfth, and propagated
from that down to the eighteenth century in copies,
every one of which underwent more or less alteration
in order to render it more intelligible, and it was in
an eighteenth century manuscript, differing in few
essentials from the copy in the *Book of Leinster*, that
I first read it. As the bards lived to please, so they
had to please to live. The popular mind only receives with pleasure and transmits with readiness
popular poetry upon the condition that it is intelligible, and hence, granting that such a man as,
say, Finn mac Cool was a real historical personage,
it is perfectly possible that some of his poetry was
handed down from generation to generation amongst

the conservative Gael, and slightly altered or modified from time to time to make it more intelligible,
according as words died out and inflexions became
obsolete. The Oriental philologist of Oxford, Max
Müller, in attempting to explain how myths arose
(according to his theory) from a disease of language,
thinks that during the transition period of which
he speaks there would be many words "understood
perhaps by the grandfather, familiar to the father, but
strange to the son, and misunderstood by the grandson." This is exactly what is taking place over half
Ireland at this very moment, and it is what has always
been at work amongst a people whose language and
literature go back with certainty for nearly 1,500 years.
Accordingly, before the art of writing became common,
ere yet expensive vellum MSS. and a highly-paid class
of historians, and schools of scribes, to a certain extent
stereotyped what they set down, it is altogether probable that people who trusted to the ear and to memory
modified and corrupted, but still handed down, at least
some famous poems, like those ascribed to Amergin or
Finn mac Cool. That the Celtic memory for things
unwritten is long I have often perceived. I have heard
from peasants, stanzas composed by Donogha More
O'Daly, Abbot of Boyle, in the thirteenth century. I
have, from an illiterate peasant, recovered, in 1890, in
Roscommon, verses which had been jotted down in
phonetic spelling in Argyleshire by Macgregor, Dean
of Lismore, in the year 1512, and which may have
been sung for hundreds of years before it struck the
fancy of the Highland divine to commit them to paper;*
and I have again heard verses in which the measure

---

* See my note on the story of Oscar du Fléau in *Revue Celtique*,
vol. 13, p. 425.

and sense were preserved, but found, on comparing
them with MSS., that several obsolete words had been
altered to others that rhymed with them and were intelligible.*   For these reasons I should be slow to
absolutely reject the authenticity of a poem simply
because the language is more modern than that of the
bard to whom it is ascribed could have been, and it
seems to me equally uncritical to either accept or
reject much of our earliest poetry, a good deal of
which may possibly be the actual (but linguisti-
cally modified) work of the supposed authors.
This modifying process is something akin to, but very
different in degree from Pope's rewriting of Dunne's
satires or Dryden's version of Chaucer, inasmuch as
it was certainly both unpremeditated and uninten-
tional.   To better understand how this modification
may have taken place, let us examine a few lines of
the thirteenth century English poem, the "Brut of
Layamon."

> "And swa ich habbe al niht
> Of mine swevene swithe ithoht
> For ich what to iwisse
> Agan is al mi blisse."

These lines were, of course, intelligible to an ordinary
Englishman at the time.   Gradually they became a
little modernized, thus :—

> And so I have all night
> Of min-e sweeven swith ythought
> For I wat to ywiss
> Agone is all my bliss.

Had these verses been preserved in folk-memory, they
must have undergone a still further modification as

---

* Cf. note on Bran's colour, at p. 277 of my *Beside the Fire*.

soon as the words sweeven (dream), swith (much) and
ywiss (certainty) began to grow obsolete, and we would
have the verse modified and mangled, perhaps something in this way,

> And so I have all the night
> Of my dream greatly thought
> For I wot and I wis
> That gone is all my bliss.

The words " I wot and I wis " in the third line represent just about as much archaism as the popular memory and taste will stand without rebelling, but even
they might be discarded and the line handed down as

> For indeed I know this
> That gone is my bliss

or something equivalent. In fact, I would venture to
say that instances of modification of language in the
direction here hinted at, may be found in two out of
every three manuscripts in the Royal Irish Academy
to-day, and just in the same sense as the lines

> For I wot and I wis
> That gone is my bliss

are Layamon's, so we may suppose

> Dubthach missi mac do Lugaid
> Laidech lantrait
> Mé ruc inmbreith etir Loegaire
> Ocus Patraic *

---

* In more modern Irish,

> Dubhthach mise, mac do Lughaidh
> Laoi-each lán-traith
> Mé rug an bhreith idir Laoghaire
> Agus Pádraig.

I.e., " I am Dubhthach, son to Lewy the lay-ful full-wise. It is

to be the fifth century O'Lugair's, or

> Leathaid folt fada fraich,
> Forbrid canach fann fionn *

to be Finn mac Cool's.

Of the many poems said to have been produced during the period we are here speaking of, none can be properly called epics or even epopees. There are few continued efforts, and the majority of the pieces though valuable for a great many reasons to students, would hardly interest an English reader when translated. The fact is, that, such a vast amount of our early literature being lost, we can only judge of what it was like through the shorter pieces which have been preserved, and even these short pieces read rather jejune and barren in English, because of the extraordinary condensation of the original—a condensation which was brought about largely by the necessity of conforming to the most rigid rules of versification. In order to see beauty in the most ancient Irish verse it is absolutely necessary to read it in the original, so as to perceive and appreciate the alliteration and other *tours de force* which appear in every line. These verses, for instance, which Mève, daughter of Conan, is said to have pronounced over Cuchorb, her husband, in the first century, appear bald enough in a literal translation :—

> Moghcorb's son conceals renown,
> Well sheds he blood by his spears,

I who delivered judgment between Lewy and Patrick." Traith is the only obsolete word here.

* In modern Irish, *leathnuighidh folt fada fraoch, i.e , leathnuighidh fraoch folt fada, foirbridh (fásaidh) canach (ceannabhán) fann fionn, i.e., spreads heath its long hair, flourishes the feeble fair cotton-grass.*

A stone over his grave—'tis a pity—
Who carried battle over Cliú Máil.

My noble king, he spoke not falsehood,
His success was certain in every danger,
As black as a raven was his brow
As sharp was his spear as a razor, etc.

One might read this kind of thing for ever in a translation without being struck by anything more than some occasional *curiosa felicitas* of phrase or picturesque expression, and one would never suspect that the original was so polished and complicated as it really is. Here are these two verses done into the exact versification of the original, in which interlinear vowel-rhymes, alliterations, and all the other requirements of the Irish are preserved and marked :—

Mochorb's son of **F**iercest **F**AME
KNown his **N**AME for bloody toil
To his **G**ory **G**rave is **G**ONE,
He who **S**HONE o'er **S**houting Moyle.

Kindly **K**ing who **L**iked not **L**IES
Rash to **R**ISE to **F**ields of **F**ame,
Raven-**B**lack his **B**rows of FEAR,
Razor-**S**harp his **S**PEAR of flame,* etc.

This specimen of Irish metre may help to place our early poetry in another light, for its beauty too often

* Here is the first verse of this in the original. The old Irish is quite unintelligible to a modern. I have here modernized the spelling :—

Mac Mogachoirb Cheileas CLÚ
Cun fearas CRU thar a gháibh
Ail uas a Ligi—budh LIACH—
Baslaide CHLIATH thar Cliú Máil.

The rhyming words do not make perfect rhyme as in English, but pretty nearly so, *clu, cru, liach, cliath, gáibh, máil.*

depends less upon the intrinsic substance of the thought than upon the external elegance of the frame-work. We must understand this in order to do justice to our very early native literature, for if any one imagines that he will find there long-sustained epics or narrative poems after the manner of the Iliad or Odyssey, or even the Nibelungenlied, or the Song of Roland, he will be very much mistaken. It consists rather of eulogies, elegies, historical poems, and lyrics, few of them of very great length, and still fewer capable of greatly interesting an English reader in a translation. Occasionally we meet with touches of nature-poetry of which the Gael has always been excessively fond. Here is a tentative translation made by O'Donovan of a part of the first poem which Finn mac Cool is said to have composed after his eating of the salmon of knowledge :—

"May-day, delightful time! How beautiful the colour! The blackbirds sing their full lay. Would that Laighay were here! The cuckoos sing in constant strains. How welcome is ever the noble brilliance of the seasons! On the margin of the branching woods the summer swallows skim the stream. The swift horses seek the pool. The heath spreads out its long hair. The weak fair bog-down grows. Sudden consternation attacks the signs; the planets, in their courses running exert an influence; the sea is lulled to rest; flowers cover the earth."

The language of this poem is so old as to be in parts unintelligible, yet he would be a bold man who would ascribe with certainty the authorship of it to Finn mac Cool in the third century, or the elegy on Cuchorb to Mève, daughter of Conan—a contemporary of Virgil and Horace. And yet all the history of this Mève is known and recorded with much apparent plausibility, and with many collateral circumstances connecting her with the men of her time. It is the same with Finn mac Cool. How much of this is real historical tradition, how much is later invention? How far can we look upon these verses as genuine? How far can we look on Finn mac Cool as an actual character? Must we at once dismiss such an idea? Of this I shall have something to say in another chapter.

In the meantime let us for the present dismiss this oldest poetry of ours, and turn to some of the most ancient prose which purports to have been composed during the same period—that is, from long before the Christian era to the coming of St. Patrick. The prose books which have come down to us as emanating from that period are not numerous. They consist for the most part of very obscure fragments of laws and law-codes.

One piece, however, is sufficiently interesting to make it worth while giving some account of it. This is the "Teagasg Flatha," or "Instructions to a Prince," alleged to have been written by Cormac mac Art for his son, Cairbre of the Liffey. Both Cormac and his son Cairbre are very great personages indeed in the romantic history of Ireland. Cormac was the son of Art the Lonely, and the grandson of Con of the Hundred Battles, and it was he who made still wider the breach with Finn mac Cool and the Fenians, which finally ended in a death struggle between them and the monarchy, in which Cairbre, —for whose instruction this book was written—was slain, and the Fenians, on the other side, almost exterminated to a man. At this time, however, we find Cairbre sitting at the feet of his father and learning wisdom—Pagan wisdom, of course, and Pagan morality, but wisdom knows neither creed nor race. The entire piece, which is of some length, is written by way of question and answer. Cairbre first puts his question to his father Cormac, and then Cormac proceeds to answer it. Here is a specimen :—

THE INSTRUCTION OF A PRINCE.

"O grandson of Con, O Cormac," said Cairbre, "what is good for a king ?"

"That is plain," said Cormac, "It is good for him to have patience and not to dispute, self-government without anger, affability without haughtiness, diligent attention to history, strict observance of covenants and agreements, strictness mitigated by mercy, in the execution of the laws," etc., etc. He proceeds thus—"It is good for him (to make) fertile land, to invite ships, to import jewels of price across sea, to purchase and bestow raiment, (to keep) vigorous swordsmen for protecting his territories, (to make) war outside his own territories, to attend the sick, to discipline his soldiers . . . let him enforce fear, let him perfect peace, (let him give) much of methaglin and wine, let him pronounce just judgments of light, let him speak all truth, for it is through the truth of a king that God gives favourable seasons."

"O grandson of Con, O Cormac," said Cairbre, "What is good for the welfare of a country ?"

"That is plain," said Cormac, "frequent convocations of sapient and good men to investigate its affairs, to abolish each evil and retain each wholesome institution, to attend to the precepts of the elders, let every assembly be convened according to law, let the law be in the hands of the nobles, let the chieftains be upright and unwilling to oppress the poor," etc., etc.

A more interesting passage is the following :—

"O grandson of Con, O Cormac, what are the duties of a prince at a banqueting house ? "

"A prince, on Samhan's Day (Nov. 1) should light his lamps and welcome his guests with clapping of hands, procure comfortable seats, the cup bearers should be respectable and active in the distribution of meat and drink. Let there be moderation of music, short stories, a welcoming countenance, a fáilte for the learned, pleasant conversations, etc. These are the duties of the prince, and the arrangement of the banqueting house."

After this follows a question which was asked often enough during the period of the Brehon law, and which for over a thousand years scarcely received another answer.

Cairbre asks, "For what qualification is a king elected over countries and tribes of people ? " and Cormac in his answer embodies the idea of every clan in Ireland in their practical choice of a leader :—

"From the goodness of his shape and family, from his experience and wisdom, from his prudence and magnanimity, from his eloquence, and bravery in battle, and from the number of his friends."

After this comes a long description of the qualifications of a prince, and Cairbre after hearing it naturally puts this question—"O descendant of Con, what was *thy* deportment when a youth ? " To which question he receives the following rather striking answer :—

"I was cheerful at the banquet of the Meecuarta,[*]

* Midh-chuarta, "house of the circulation of mead," was the name of a magnificent central building at Tara.

fierce in battle, but vigilant and circumspect. I was kind
to friends, a physician to the sick, merciful towards the
weak, stern towards the headstrong. Although possessed of knowledge I was inclined towards taciturnity.
Although strong I was not haughty. I mocked not
the old, although I was young. I was not vain,
although I was valiant. When I spoke of a person in
his absence I praised, not defamed, him, for it is by
these customs that we are known to be courteous and
civilised (*riaghalach*)."

There is an extremely beautiful answer given later
on by Cormac to the rather simple question of his
son,—" O grandson of Con, what is good for
me?"

"If thou attend to my command," answers Cormac,
" thou wilt not mock the old, although thou art young,
nor the poor although thou art well-clad, nor the lame
although thou art agile, nor the blind although thou
art clear-sighted, nor the feeble although thou art
strong, nor the ignorant although thou art learned.
Be not slothful, nor passionate, nor penurious, nor
idle, nor jealous, for he who is so is an object of hatred
to God as well as to man."

" O grandson of Con," asks Cairbre in another
place, "I would fain know how I am to conduct
myself among the wise and among the foolish, among
friends and among strangers, among old and among
young?" And to this question his father gives the
following notable response :—

" Be not too knowing nor too simple, be not proud,
be not inactive, be not too humble nor yet haughty;
be not talkative but be not too silent; be not timid
neither be severe. For if thou shouldst appear too
knowing thou wouldst be satirised and abused ; if too
simple thou wouldst be imposed upon ; if too proud

thou wouldst be shunned; if too humble thy dignity would suffer ; if talkative thou wouldst not be deemed learned ; if too severe thy character would be defamed ; if too timid thy rights would be encroached upon."

To the curious question, " O grandson of Con, what are the most lasting things in the world ?" the equally curious answer is returned, " Grass, copper, and yew." Of women King Cormac has nothing good to say. Possibly monarchs, from Solomon down, have not been in a position to judge the sex impartially or objectively. At least to the question, " O grandson of Con, how shall I distinguish the characters of women ?" the following bitter answer is given :—

" I know them, but I cannot describe them. Their counsel is foolish, they are forgetful of love, most headstrong in their desires, fond of folly, prone to enter rashly into engagements, given to swearing, proud to be asked in marriage, tenacious of enmity, cheerless at the banquet, rejectors of reconciliation, prone to strife, of much garrulity—until evil be good, until hell be heaven, until the sun hide his light, until the stars of heaven fall, women will remain as we have stated. Woe to him, my son, who desires or serves a bad woman, woe to every one who has got a bad wife."

This Christian allusion to heaven and hell, and some other passages, show that the tract as we have it at present, despite a certain Pagan flavouring in parts, cannot be in its entirety the work of King Art or of his son, but it may very well be the embodiment and extension of an early genuine Pagan discourse ; because after Christianity had succeeded in gaining the upper hand over Paganism, a kind of tacit compromise seems to have been arrived at, by means of which the bards and filès and representatives of the old Pagan learning were allowed to continue to propagate their stories, tales, poems, and genealogies at the price of tacking on to them a little Christian admixture, just as the vessels of some feudatory nation are compelled to fly at the mast-head the flag of the suzerain power. But so badly has the dove-tailing of the Christian on to the Pagan part been performed in most of the oldest romances, that the pieces come away quite separate in the hands of even the least skilled analyser, and the Pagan substratum stands forth entirely distinct from the Christian accretion.

CHAPTER IV.

I' is this easy analysis of our early literature into its ante-Christian and its post-
Christian elements which makes it so
valuable. For when all spurious accretions
have been stripped off, we find in our
most ancient tales a genuine picture of
Pagan life in Europe, for which we look
in vain elsewhere. In fact, he who would
examine the early state of society over a
large part of our continent is forced to
see it through coloured glasses, in other words to view
it through the prejudiced medium of the Greeks and
Romans, to whom everyone outside of themselves was
a barbarian. He has no other means of estimating what were the social life, feelings, and modes of
thought, of those great races who inhabited so large
a part of the old world, Gaul, Belgium, North
Italy, parts of Germany, Spain, Switzerland, and the
British Isles, who burned Rome in its infancy, who
plundered Greece, and who colonized Asia Minor.
But, in the early Irish romances and historical tales

he sees come to light another standard, by which to measure; through this early Irish peep-hole he gets a vivid picture of the life and manners of the race in one of its strongholds, from which he may conjecture, and even assume a good deal with regard to the others.

That the pictures of social life and early society drawn in the Irish romances represent phases not common to the Irish alone, but to large portions of that Celtic race which once owned half Europe, may be surmised with something like certainty from the way in which characteristics of the "Celts," barely mentioned by Greek and Roman writers, re-appear amongst ourselves in all the intimate detail and fond expansion of romance.   Let us glance at a few.

Posidonius, who was a friend of Cicero and wrote some hundred years before Christ, mentions that there was a custom at that time in Gaul, of fighting at a feast for the best bit which was to be given to the most valiant warrior.   The custom thus briefly noticed by this writer might be passed unheeded by the ordinary reader, but not so by the Irish one.   He will remember the early romances of his race, in which the *curadh-mir*, or "heroes-bit" figures.   He will remember that it is upon this custom one of the most celebrated of ancient Irish romances—the Feast of Bricriu—hinges.   It opens thus : Bricriu was one who always delighted in setting the Ultonians by the ears and provoking blows, quarrels, and jealousy wherever he went.   Upon this occasion he had built a new and magnificent house.   "The dining hall" says the eleventh century text of this certainly pre-Christian story, "was built like that of the High King at Tara. From the hearth to the wall were nine beds, and each of the side walls was thirty-five feet high and covered with ornaments of gilt bronze. Against one of the side

walls of that palace was reared a royal bed destined
for Conor,* King of Ulster, which looked down upon
all the others.   It was ornamented with precious stones,
carbuncles, and other gems of great value.   The gold
and silver, and all sorts of jewellery which covered that
bed shone with such splendour that the night was as
brilliant as the day."   The story goes on to relate how
when Bricriu had finished building his new palace and
had laid by a great store of provisions, furniture, bed-
coverings, and everything necessary, he started off to
visit Conor, King of Ulster, at his Court in Emania.†
"To Conor," says our history, "he addressed his
speech, and to the rest of the Ultonians.‡   "Come
visit me," said he, "you will have a feast which I offer
you."   "I consent," said Conor, "if the Ultonians

---

* In the old texts this name is written Concobar, in the modern
language Conchúbhair, which is, strange to say, usually pronounced not "Cun-hoo-war" or "Cun-hoor" as spelt (whence
the English form Conor), but Cruch-hoor (the ch is guttural)
whence Banim's "*Crohore* of the Bill-hook." I have preferred
to keep the English form Conor, but in ancient times the b was
certainly pronounced, though there are traces of its pronunciation
being lost as early as the twelfth century. With curious conservatism it has been retained to this day in the spelling. Zimmer
says he finds it spelt Conchor in the twelfth century book, the
Liber Landavensis, from which of course, Cnochor followed by
easy metathesis, but as "cn" is pronounced in the West of Ireland
as "cr" (Cf. cnoc cno for cnoc cno, etc.) the present pronunciation
arose.

The conservatism of Irish spelling is wonderful. Zimmer remarks elsewhere (*Keltische Studien*, Heft I., 51) that "already
in the oldest Middle Irish MSS. from the beginning of the twelfth
century, the orthography, as far as the consonants go, is purely
historical, and one which represents the speech of the seventh
century, or of even a still earlier period."

† In Irish Emain-Macha, generally Latinized Emania.

‡ *I.e.*, "the people of Ulster," from Ultonia, the Latin form
of the Irish Uladh = Ulster.

do." But, Fergus mac Roy and the other nobles of Ulster replied : " we will not go, for if we do go to take part in the feast to which we are invited, Bricriu would excite quarrels amongst us, and the number of the dead amongst us would be greater than the number of the living." "If ye do not come to me," said Bricriu, " what I shall do to ye shall be still worse." "What then will you do?" asked Conor, "if the Ultonians do not come?" "I shall excite," said Bricriu, "quarrels amongst the kings, the chiefs, the illustrious warriors, and the young nobles; they shall kill each other amongst themselves if they come not to drink ale at my feast." "We shall never kill ourselves for you," said Conor. Bricriu answered, "I shall embroil fathers and sons; they shall slay each other mutually. If I succeed not in bringing you to my house I shall put discord between the mothers and the daughters. If I succeed not in bringing you with me I shall provoke a quarrel between the two breasts of every woman; their breasts shall crush one the other. They shall rot; they shall die."

"Verily," said Fergus mac Roy, " it is better for us to go."

" Let the question be deliberated on," said Sencha,* son of Ailill, "let a small number of chiefs examine and see if it be good to accept the invitation."

"It would be wrong," said Conor, "not to study the matter in council."

The nobles then proceeded to discuss the matter, and they arrived at the conclusion to adopt the advice of Sencha, "but," said Sencha, "since

---

* Sencha is the wise man *par excellence*, the Nestor of the Ultonian cycle of tales. He was a lawyer and Brehon, and always spoke wisdom and made up quarrels.

ye must go to Bricriu, choose ye sureties who shall guarantee his good conduct, and place round him eight men with swords, who shall surround him every time he issues from the house, and that supervision of him shall commence from the time of his showing you the preparations of his feast." Conor's son brought this answer to Bricriu, and told him of the discussion that had preceded it. "I am satisfied," said Bricriu; "let it be so."

The Ultonians thereupon set out from Emania, each band round its chief, each company round its prince, and each battalion round its king; and noble and splendid was the march of the warriors and heroes as they advanced towards the palace of Bricriu.

The story goes on to relate how Bricriu planned in his own mind how to excite a quarrel amongst the Ultonians despite their precautions, and how he secretly took Lewy the Vanquisher aside, and after much flattering asked him why it was that he did not always receive the *curadh-mir*, or hero's bit, at Emania. "If it is I who should have it," said Lewy, "I shall have it."

"I shall make you obtain first place amongst the warriors of Ireland," said Bricriu, "if you follow my counsel. If you get the hero's bit at my house now, you shall also get it at Emania. You will do well to obtain the hero's bit in my house."

After this he describes what his munificent *curadh-mir* consisted of—a seven-year-old pig and a seven-year-old cow that had been fed on milk and corn and the finest food since their birth, a hundred cakes of corn cooked with honey,—and every four cakes took one sack of corn to make it,—and a vat of wine large enough to hold three of the warriors of the Ultonians.

"Since, then," said Bricriu, "it is you who are the best of the warriors of Ulster, it is to you they ought to give that morsel, and it is for you I have desired it; consequently, when the last day's feast is ready, let your charioteer rise up and demand it, and it is to you the hero's morsel shall be given."

"There shall be men slain on that day," answered Lewy, " or my wish shall be gratified."

Afterwards Bricriu went in search of Conall Cearnach, and bestowed much flattery upon him, telling him that to himself the hero's bit shall be given. Bricriu, remarks the narrator, had flattered Lewy well: he flattered Conall Cearnach twice as much. Afterwards he sought Cuchulain, and so won upon him that the great hero exclaimed—"I swear it by the oath men swear in my nation, he shall be without a head who shall come to dispute the hero's bit with me."

Upon this opening, and the decision about the hero-bit, depends all the subsequent romance.

Such is the air of reality which the Irish reciter throws round the old manners and customs of the race, and such the ruddy covering of flesh and blood in which we find the dry bones of Posidonius and Cæsar revived in the old Irish literature.

Again, we see in Cæsar that the Gauls did not fight in chariots when he invaded them ; although it is recorded that they did so fight two hundred years before his time, even as the Persians fought against the Greeks, and as the Greeks themselves must have done still further back. But in Ireland we find this epic mode of warfare in full force. Every great man has his charioteer; they fight from their cars as in Homeric days, and much is told us of both steeds, chariot, and driver. In the romance of Bricriu's Feast it is the three charioteers of the three warriors who claim the hero's bit for their masters, since these are apparently ashamed to make the first move themselves. The charioteer was more than a mere servant. Cuchulain sometimes called his charioteer "friend" or "master" (popa), and, on the occasion of his fight with Ferdia, desires him, in case he (Cuchulain) should show signs of yielding, to "excite, reproach, and speak evil to me, so that the ire of my rage and anger shall grow the more on me; but if he give ground before me, thou shalt laud me and praise me and speak good words to me, that my courage may be the greater," and this command his friend and charioteer punctually executed.

The chariot itself is in many places graphically described. Here is how its approach is portrayed in the Táin :—" It was not long," says the chronicler, "until Ferdia's charioteer heard the noise approaching, the clamour and the rattle and the whistling and the tramp and the thunder and the clatter and the roar, namely, the shield-noise of the light shields, and the hissing of the spears and the loud clangour of the swords and the tinkling of the helmet, and the ringing of the armour, and the friction of the arms; the dangling of the missive weapons, the straining of the ropes, and the loud clattering of the wheels, and the creaking of the chariot, and the trampling of the horses, and the triumphant advance of the champion and the warrior towards the ford approaching him."

In the romance called the "Intoxication of the Ultonians," it is mentioned that they drove so fast in the wake of Cuchulain that "the iron wheels of the chariots cut the roots of the immense trees." Here is how the romancist describes the advance of such a body upon Tara-Luachra :—

" Not long were they there, the two watchers and the two druids, until a full fierce rush of the first band broke hither past the glen. Such was the fury with which they advanced that there was not left a spear on a rack nor a shield on a spike nor a sword in an armoury in Tara-Luachra that did not fall down. From every house on which was thatch in Tara-Luachra it fell in immense flakes. One would think that it was the sea that had come over the walls and over the corners of the world upon them. The forms of countenances were changed, and there was chattering of teeth in Tara-Luachra within. The two druids fell in fits and in faintings and in paroxysms, one of them out over the wall, and the other over the wall inside."

Descriptions like this are constantly occurring in the tales, and enable us to better realise the heroic period of warfare, and to fill up in our imagination many a long-regretted lacuna in our knowledge of primitive Europe.

"Those philosophers" (says Diodorus Siculus, a Greek writer of the Augustine age, speaking of the Druids) "like the lyric poets called bards, have a great authority both in affairs of peace and war; friends and enemies listen to them. Also when the two armies are in presence of one another, and swords drawn and spears couched, they throw themselves into the midst of the combatants and appease them as though they were charming wild beasts. Thus, even amongst the most savage barbarians anger submits to the rule of wisdom, and the god of war pays homage to the Muses." To show that the manners and customs of the Keltoi or Celts of whom Diodorus speaks were in this respect identical with those of their Irish cousins (or brothers), and to give another instance of the warm light shed by Irish literature upon the early customs of Western Europe, I shall convert the abstract into the concrete by a page or two from an Irish romance, not an old one,* but one which, no doubt, preserves many original traditionary traits. In this story Finn mac Cool† at a great feast in his castle at Allen, asks Goll about some tribute which he claimed, and is dissatisfied at the answer of Goll, who may be called the Ajax of the Fenians. After that there arose a quarrel at the feast, the beginning of which is thus graphically portrayed :—

" Goll," said Finn, " you have acknowledged in that speech that you came from the city of Beirbhe to the battle of Cnoca, and that you slew my father there, and it is a bold and disobedient thing of you to tell me that," said Finn.

" By my hand, O Finn," said Goll, " If you were to dishonour me as your father did, I would give you the same payment that I gave Cool."

" Goll," said Finn, " I would be well able not to let that word pass with you, for I have a hundred valiant warriors in my following for every one that is in yours."

" Your father had that also," said Goll, " and yet I

---

* I translated this from a manuscript in my possession made by one Patrick O'Prunty (an ancestor probably of Charlotte Brontë) in 1763. Mr. Standish Hayes O'Grady has since published a somewhat different text of it.

† In Irish Fionn mac Cúmhail, pronounced Finn (or Fewn in Munster) mac Coo-will or Cool.

E

avenged my dishonour on him, and I would do the same to you if you were to deserve it of me."

White-skinned Carroll O'Baoisgne* spoke, and 'tis what he said—"O Goll," said he, "there is many a man," said he, "to silence you and your people in the household of Finn mac Cool."

Bald, cursing Conan mac Morna spoke, and 'tis what he said—"I swear by my arms of valour," said he, "that Goll, the day he has least men, has a man and a hundred in his household, and not a man of them but would silence you."

"Are you one of those, peryerse, bald-headed Conan?" said Carroll.

"I am one of them, black-visaged, nail-torn, skin-scratched, little-strength Carroll," says Conan, "and I would soon prove it to you that Cool was in the wrong."

It was then that Carroll arose, and he struck a daring fist, quick and ready, upon Conan, and there was no submission in Conan's answer, for he struck the second fist on Carroll in the middle of his face and his teeth.

After this the chronicler relates how first one joined in and then another, until at last all the adherents of Goll and Finn, and even the captains themselves are hard at work. "After that," he adds, "bad was the place for a mild smooth-fingered woman, or a weak or infirm person, or an aged long-lived elder." This fight continued "from the beginning of the night till the rising of the sun in the morning," and was only stopped—just as Diodorus says, battles were stopped—by the intervention of the bards. "It

* Pronounced Bweesg-nă, the tripthong aoi is always pronounced like *ee* in Irish.

was then," says the romancist, "that the prophesying poet of the pointed words, that guerdon-ful good man of song, Fergus Finnbheóil, rose up, and all the Fenians' men of science along with him, and they sang their hymns and good poems, and their perfect lays to those heroes to silence and to soften them.   It was then they ceased from their slaughtering and maiming, on hearing the music of the poets, and they let their weapons fall to earth, and the poets took up their weapons and they went between them, and grasped them with the grasp of reconciliation."   When the palace was cleared it was found that 1,100 of Finn's people had been killed between men and women, and eleven men and fifty women of Goll's party.

Cæsar speaks of the numbers who frequented the schools of the Druids in Gaul.   " It is said," he adds, " that they learn there a great number of verses, and that is why some of these pupils spend twenty years in learning.   It is not, according to the Druids, permissible to entrust verses to writing, although they use the Greek alphabet in all other affairs, public and private."   Of this prohibition to commit their verses to paper we have no trace, so far as I know, in our literature, but the accounts of the early bardic schools entirely bear out the description here given of them by Cæsar, and again show the solidarity of custom which seems to have existed between the various Celtic tribes.   According to our early manuscripts, it took from nine to twelve years for a student to take the highest degree at the bardic schools, and in many cases where the pupil failed to master sufficiently the subjects of the year, he had probably to spend two over it, so that it is quite possible that some might easily spend twenty years

over their learning before arriving at the highest degree.   And much of this learning was, as
Cæsar notes, in verse.   All our earlier law tracts
appear to have been so, and even all our earliest
romances.   There is a very interesting account extant
called the "Proceedings of the Great Bardic Associa-
tion," which leads up to the epic of the Táin Bo
Chuailgne, the greatest of the Irish romances,
according to which this great tale was at one
time lost, and the great Bardic Institution was
commanded to hunt for and recover it.   The fact of
its being said that the perfect tale was lost for ever,
"and that only a fragmentary and broken form of it
would go down to posterity," undoubtedly means, as
has been pointed out by Sullivan, "that the filling
up the gaps in the poem by prose narrative is
meant."   In point of fact the tale, as we have it
now, consists half of verse and half of prose.
Nor is this peculiar to the Táin.   All our oldest
and many of our modern tales are composed in this
way.   In most or all cases the verse is of a more
archaic character, and more difficult than the prose.
In very many romances an expanded prose narrative of several pages is followed by a more condensed poem saying the same thing.   So much did
the Irish at last come to look upon it as a matter
of course that every romance should be interspersed
with poetry, that even writers of the seventeenth and
eighteenth centuries, who consciously invented their
stories, as a modern novelist invents his, have interspersed their pieces with passages in verse as did
Comyn in his Turlough Mac Stairn ; as did the author
of the Son of Ill-counsel, the author of the Parlia-
ment of Clan Lopus, and others.   We may perhaps
take it, then, that in the earliest days all our romances

were composed in verse, and learned by heart by the students—possibly before the alphabet was known at all ; afterwards, when lacunæ occurred through defective memory on the part of the reciter, he filled up the gaps with prose. Those who committed to paper our earliest tales wrote down as much of the old poetry as they could recollect or had access to, and wrote the connecting narrative in prose. Hence, it soon came to pass that if a story pretended to any antiquity, it must be interspersed with verses ; and at last it happened that the Irish taste became so conformed to this style of writing, that authors adopted it, as I have said, even in the seventeenth and eighteenth century.

This chapter has been written with a view to show that the study of Irish literature is one elevated above mere provinciality or even nationality. I wish to show that those of the great nations of to-day, whose ancestors were mostly Celts, but whose language, literature, and traditions have completely disappeared, can best form an idea of their own past of which nothing exists, by studying the records of the Irish past, of which such a quantity still remains. When we find so much of the brief information given us by the classical writers concerning the Celts with whom they came in contact, not only borne out, but so amply illustrated by old Irish literature, it is not very rash to argue that, in other matters too, the races bore to each other a very close resemblance.

Much more could be advanced upon this point, as that the four Gallo-Roman inscriptions to Brigantia found in Great Britain, are really to Brigit, a goddess of the Irish, that the Brennus who burned Rome, 390 years B.C., and the Brennus who stormed Delphi 110 years later, were only the god Brian,* son of the

* Who also figures in the "Three Sorrows of Story-telling."

goddess Brigit, under whose tutelage the Gaels marched, that Lugu-dunum, afterwards Lug-dunum, now Lyon, is so-called from the god Lugh the Long-handed, to whom two Celtic inscriptions are found, one in Spain, one in Switzerland; but enough has been said upon this point, and those who are curious upon the matter may look up the erudite pages of Monsieur de Jubainville, to whom all Irishmen should owe a lasting debt of gratitude for the more than Gallic luminousness with which he has sought to disentangle the web of our early mythology.

CHAPTER V.

EARLY IRISH ROMANCES.

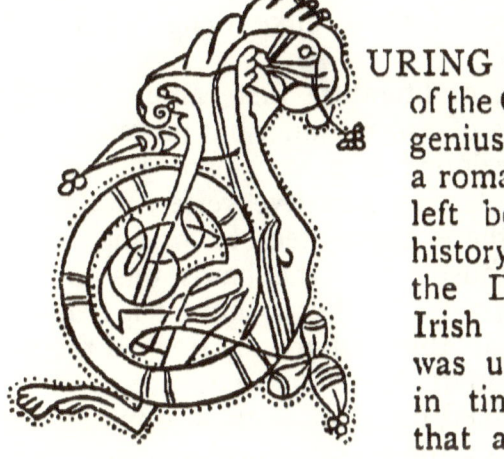URING the golden period of the Greek and Roman genius no one ever wrote a romance. Epics they left behind them, and history, but the romance, the Danish Saga, the Irish sgeul or úrsgeul was unknown. It was in time of decadence that a body of Greek prose romance appeared, and the Latin language produced in this line little of a higher character than such books as the *Gesta Romanorum.* In Greece and Italy, where the genial climate favoured all kinds of open air representations the great development of the drama took the place of novelistic literature, as it did for a long time amongst the English after the Elizabethan revival. In Ireland, on the other hand, the dramatic stage was never reached at all, but the development of the úrsgeul, romance, or novel, was

quite abnormally great. One of our popular lecturers
has asserted, if I mistake not, that the dramatic is an
inevitable, and I think he says, an early development in
the history of every literature, but this is to generalize
from insufficient instances.   The Irish literature which
kept on developing—to some extent at least—for over
a thousand years, and of which 1,000 volumes still
exist, never evolved a drama, nor, as far as I know,
so much as a miracle play, although these are found
in Welsh and even Cornish.

What Ireland did produce—and produce nobly and
well—was romance.   From the first to the last, from
the seventh to the seventeenth century, Irishmen,
without distinction of class, alike delighted in the
úrsgeul.

When this form of literature first came into vogue
we have no means of ascertaining, but narrative prose
was probably developed at a very early period as a
supplement to defective narrative verse ; not that it
were then and there committed to writing, for it
appears that the business of the bards was to learn
their stories by heart. I take it, however, that they
did not actually do this, but merely learned the incidents of a story in their regular sequence, and that
their training enabled them to fill them up and clothe
them on the spur of the moment in the most effective
garments, decking them out with passages of gaudy
description, with rattling alliterative lines and "runs,"
and with abundance of adjectival declamation. The
bards, no matter from what quarter of the island, had
all to know the same story or novel, provided it was a
renowned one ; with each the sequence of incidents, and
the incidents themselves, were probably for a long time
the same, but the language in which they were tricked
out and the length to which they were spun, depended

probably upon the genius or bent of each particular
bard.   Of course in process of time divergences began
to arise, and hence came different versions of the same
story.   That, at least, is how I account for such passages as " but others say that it was not there he was
killed, but in," etc. ; " but some of the books say that
it was not on that wise it happened but thus," and
so on.

It is probable that very many novels were in existence before the coming of St. Patrick, but highly
improbable that they were at that time written down
at full length.   It was I think only after the country
had become Christianised and full of schools of learning, that the bards experienced the desire of writing
down their sagas, with as much as they could recapture
of the ancient poetry upon which they were built.   In
the *Book of Leinster*, a manuscript of the early twelfth
century, we find in a list the names of 187 of those romances, with 350 of which an ollamh (ollav) had to be
acquainted.   The ollamh was the highest dignitary
amongst the bards, and it took him from nine to
twelve years' training to learn the 250 prime stories
and the 100 secondary ones, along with the other
things which were required of him.   The prime stories,—the novels of the time, for they were nothing
more nor less,—are divided in the manuscripts into
the following romantic catalogue :—Destructions or
Fortified Places, Cow Spoils (*i.e.*, cattle raiding expeditions), Courtships or Wooings, Battles, Cave
Stories, Navigations, Tragical Deaths, Feasts, Sieges,
Adventures, Elopements, Slaughters, Water-eruptions,
Expeditions, Progresses, and Visions.   " He is no
poet," says the *Book of Leinster*, " who does not
synchronize and harmonise all the stories."   We
have, as I have said, the names of 187 such stories

in that book, and the names of many more are given in the tenth or eleventh century tale of Mac Coise, and all the known ones, with the exception of one tale added later on, and one which evidently through an error in transcription is made to refer to Arthur instead of Aithirne, are about events prior to the year 650 or thereabouts. We may take it, then, that this list was drawn up in the seventh century.

Now who were the authors of these couple of hundred romances? It is a natural question but one which cannot be answered. There is not a trace of their authorship remaining, if authorship be the right word for what I suspect to have been the gradual growth of racial tribal and family history, mixed with Celtic mythology, thus forming stories which were ever being told and retold, and polished up, and added to, and which were—some of them—handed down for perhaps countless generations; others recount historical tribal or family doings, magnified during the course of time; others again of more recent date give us perhaps fairly accurate accounts of real events. I take it that as soon as bardic schools and colleges began to be formed, there was no class of learning more popular than that which taught the great traditionary stories of the various tribes and families of the great Gaelic race, and the intercommunication between the bardic colleges propagated local tradition throughout all Ireland.

The very essence of the national life of Erin was embodied in these stories, but unfortunately few only out of the enormous mass have survived down to our day, and these mostly mutilated or preserved in mere digests. Some, however, exist at nearly full length, quite sufficient to show us what the romances were like, and to cause us to regret the irreparable

loss inflicted upon our race by the ravages of Danes,
Normans, and English. Even as it is, O'Curry asserts
that the contents of the strictly historical tales known
to him would be sufficient to fill up 4,000 of the
enormous pages of the Four Masters. He computed
that the tales about Finn, Ossian, and the Fenians
would alone fill another 3,000 pages. In addition
to these we have an extraordinary number of ima-
ginative stories, neither historical nor Fenian, such
as the *Three Sorrows of Story-telling* and the like,
sufficient to fill 5,000 pages more, not to speak of
the more recent novel-like productions of the later
Irish.

Omitting for the present local and tribal stories,
we find that there are three great classes of national
romance or saga, common to the whole nation. These
are, first, the mythological cycle about the Tuatha
de Danann, Firbolgs, Fomorians, the Dagda, etc.,
secondly, the Cycle of Cuchulain and the Red
Branch, and thirdly, the Fenian or Ossianic cycle.
We must discuss each of these separately. To these
three we might possibly add a fourth cycle, which exists
not indeed on paper, but in the popular recollection,
that of the Elves or Fairies. We thus come by a re-
gular dwarfing process from Gods to Heroes ($\delta\alpha\iota\mu o\nu\epsilon\varsigma$),
from Heroes to Men, and from Men to Elves. Of
these last, however, we shall have nothing to say in this
volume.*

---

* I have collected some thirty stories in Irish amongst the
peasantry, the nucleus of a Fairy Cycle.

CHAPTER VI.

THE MYTHOLOGICAL CYCLE.

HE stories which fall under the head of the mythological cycle are both fewer in number and more confused in substance than those of the other two cycles. To antiquarians and etymologists, however, they are the most interesting of all, for it is in them we find the clearest traces of the old Irish pantheon. In other words we can, to a certain extent, make acquaintance with the gods of the early Irish, as we make acquaintance with those of Greece, Rome, and Scandinavia, in classical literature and northern saga. We cannot do this at first sight as we can with the classical gods. On the contrary, one might read through Irish literature and scarcely see that it contained a mythology at all. The reason of this is that at a very early period the Irish forgot that these beings and races of whom they still continued to tell, were the gods and demi-gods of their ancestors, until at last their historians came to speak of them as though they were ordinary tribes and ordinary men.

This process of treatment is called Euhemerism from
a Greek writer of the fourth century, B.C., named
Euhemerus who attempted to do the same thing by
the Greeks.   Occasionally, indeed, a fairy being,
generally a Tuatha de Danann stands out in the ordinary romances, as Angus of the Brugh in *Diarmuid
and Gráinne*, who saves his protegé Diarmuid very
much like a Deus ex machina, and who when that
hero is at length slain brings him to his palace of the
Brugh on the Boyne, and says, "since I cannot restore
him to life I will send a soul into him so that he may
talk to me every day."   But, upon the whole, while
there occurs a good deal about wizardry and the Shee*
men and women who inhabit the fairy shees or hills,
and the incantations of Druids, there is little or nothing
about a so-called race of gods, for the simple reason that
the gods came to be treated as men, and the Firbolgs,
Fomorians, Fir-Domnans, Fir-Galeons, Tuatha de
Dananns, etc., are spoken of, both by annalists and historians, as ordinary human tribes.   Indeed, Keating in
enumerating the chief men of the Tuatha de Dananns
the Dagda, Manannán and the rest, actually adds "and
these were their three goddesses, Badb, Macha, and
Morighan," quite unsuspicious of the probable fact
that the Dagda himself was a kind of Irish Jupiter
and Manannán an Irish Neptune, just as much gods
of the ancient Irish as the Morighan (the war-goddess)
herself.   Of course, all these races and names are
fitted into the annals each in a place—I suppose I
must call it an invented place—of its own, and the
intervals filled up with the names of kings who are

* The Irish *sidhe*, equivalent to "Fairy"; these were generally believed to be the Tuatha de Dananns who disappeared
from before the Milesians and lived *inside* the hills.

said to have reigned over Erin and died. The
Dagda himself dies, slain in the battle of North
Moytura by a spear cast at him by Kethlen,* the
wife of Balor the Fomorian of the Evil Eye, from
whom Enniskillen is said to take its name. The
great Lugh or Lughaidh,* from whom Lyons (Lug-
dunum), no doubt, takes its name, and to whom are
found early Celtic inscriptions is slain also. So is
Manannán, so is Ogma—no doubt the Gaulish Heracles 'Ogmios'—and so are the rest, like so many
human beings. But all this arose, first from the
rationalizing or euhemerizing tendencies of the early
Irish, and secondly from the desire of the mediæval-
ists to trace back the history and kings of Ireland
to Adam, after the fashion of the Hebrew pedigrees
with which the introduction of Christianity made
them acquainted.

The mythological cycle of tales tells us how the
Nemedians, or children of Nemedh, colonized Ireland,
and how they were oppressed by the Fomorians, who
are generally described as African sea-robbers, and
how the two races nearly exterminated each other at
the fight round the tower of Conning on Tory Island.†
Some of the Nemedians survived and fled away, taking
refuge in Greece ; and a couple of hundred years later,
being driven out of Greece, they came back again,
calling themselves Firbolg, i.e., " sack" or "bag men."
It was after they had held the island in peace for thirty
or forty years that the celebrated Tuatha de Danann ʟ
came in. They, too, were Nemedians who had left
Ireland after that same fight at Conning's Tower. They,
too, like the Firbolg, had been—some say in Greece—for

* Pronounced Kellen and Lewy.
† The account in Nennius is something different.

a period of exile, which endured about thirty-five years longer than that of the Firbolg. On their return to Ireland they found the Firbolg there before them, and were greatly surprised to hear them talk the same Gaelic language as themselves. They offered to divide the island, but the Firbolg would not have it, so the de Dananns fought the battle of North Moytura with them, and beat them. Thirty years later they fought the second battle of South Moytura against the Fomorians, who had once more waxed strong, and beat them also. They held the island after this for about two hundred years, until the coming of the Scots or Gaels, or Milesians, as they are variously called, who in their turn beat the Tuatha de Dananns, and reigned here in their stead until conquered by the English.* The first and second battles of Moytura† are told at length in two prose epics, both

---

* It is worth noting in this place, as a mark of the persistent continuity of our history, that after being beaten here the Firbolg fled to the islands, and colonized Aran and Islay and Rachlin and the Hebrides. Long afterwards, at the time when Ireland was divided into five provinces, the Cruithnigh or Picts drove them out of the islands, and they were forced to come back to Ireland to Cairbre Niafer, King of Leinster, who allotted them a territory, but put such a rack rent upon them, that they were glad to fly into Connacht, where Ollioll and Mève, the king and queen who figure in the Ultonian cycle, gave them a free grant of land, and there Duald Mac Firbis, two hundred and fifty years ago found their descendants in plenty. According to some accounts, however, the Firbolg were never at any time wholly driven out of Connacht, and if they are a real race they still form the basis of the population there. Máine Mór, ancestor of the O'Kellys is said to have wrested from them the territory of Ui Maine (part of Roscommon and Galway) in the 6th century.

† When the oldest lists of romances were drawn up there was only one battle of Moytura known, or at least mentioned, that was evidently the one against the Fomorians, now called the second battle. In the more recent list contained in the Intro-

of them interesting ; the second especially so, it being the account of the battle in which the Tuatha de Danann defeated the Fomorians, after a seven-year preparation for the fight.   There are traits in this account which evidently show the mythological origin of all the characters.   Just as the most contradictory accounts of Zeus are met with in Greek mythology, some glorifying him as reigning in Olympus supreme over gods and men, others representing him as playing low and indecent tricks tranformed in the guise of a cuckoo or a bull, so we find the Dagda (whose real name is said to have been Eochaidh* the Ollamh) at one time high-king of the whole de Danann race, and organizer of victory, and at another in a far less dignified and clearly mythological position.   Here, for instance, is the account of his visit to the camp of the Fomorians, in order to cause them to lose time and to put them off with talk until the de Danann should have their armaments ready.   I give this passage not at all as a specimen of one of the most interesting romances of the cycle that we have, but simply as a proof of how the mythological character of the heroes, though nearly lost throughout many parts of the tale, is clearly preserved in this, where the great Dagda is seen, like Zeus at times, in a most unprepossessing position.

" When the Dagda† had come to the camp of the Fomorians he demanded a truce, and he obtained it. The Fomorians prepared a porridge for him ; it was

---

duction to the *Senchus Mór* (p. 46, Master of the Rolls Series) there is mention made of both battles.   There is only a single copy of each of these stories known to be extant—of how many fine stories has even the last copy perished !

* Yohee the ollav, or ullav.

† Jubainville thinks this name = Dago-dêvo-s, " the Good God."

to ridicule him they did this, for he greatly loved porridge. They filled for him the king's cauldron, which was five hand-breadths in depth. They threw into it eighty pots of milk and a proportionate quantity of meal and fat, with goats and sheep and swine, which they got cooked along with the rest. Then they poured the broth into a hole dug in the ground, 'Unless you eat all that's there,' said Indech to him, 'you shall be put to death, we don't want you to be reproaching us, and we must satisfy you." The Dagda took the spoon ; it was so great that in the hollow of it a man and a woman might be contained. The pieces which went into that spoon were halves of salted pigs and quarters of bacon. The Dagda said, 'Here is good eating, if the broth be as good as its odour,' and as he carried the spoonful to his mouth, he said, "The proverb is true that the good cooking is not spoiled by the bad pot.'*

"When he had finished he scraped the ground with his finger to the very bottom of the hole to take what remained of it, and after that he went to sleep to digest his soup. His stomach was greater than the greatest cauldron in large houses, and the Fomorians mocked at him.

"He went away, and came to the bank of the Eba. He did not walk with ease, so large was his stomach. He was dressed in very bad guise. He had a cape which scarcely reached below his shoulders. Beneath that cloak was seen a brown mantle, which descended no lower than his hips. It was cut away above, and very large in the breast. His two shoes were of horses skin, with the hair outside. He held a wheeled fork,

---

* Thus perilously translated by Jubainville. Stokes does not attempt it.

F

which would have been heavy enough for eight men,
and he let it trail behind him.   It dug a furrow deep
enough and large enough to become the frontier mearn
between two provinces.   Therefore it is called the
track of the Dagda's club."

In the Tuatha de Danann cycle we discern clearly
enough the figures of Badhb (Birc) the Irish Bellona,
Diancécht the Esculapius, Ogma the strong man, who
is, of course, the Gaulish god Ogmius, of whom Lucian
gives so curious an account, and whom he equates at
once with Hermes and Heracles, although he is with
us figured as a powerful rather than as a persuasive
man ; Brian and his brothers ; Lugh the Longhanded,
otherwise called the Ildana, or man of many sciences,
the Irish Apollo ; Brigit, the Goddess of Poets, or the
Irish muse, from whose identity many attributes have
doubtless passed over to the credit of her namesake,
the Nun of Kildare ; Dana, the mother of the gods,
who was married to Bres the Fomorian, and appears
identical with Brigit ; Manannán, the Gaelic Neptune, and many others.   All this early history, if not
wholly mythological, and the outcome of a past belief
in a race of good Gods (the Tuatha de Dananns) and
bad spirits (the Fomorians, etc.) is certainly closely
bound up with it, and Jubainville sees in the coloniza-
tion of Partholan, the children of Nemedh, and the
Tuatha de Dananns, an Irish version of the Greek ages
of gold, silver and brass, just as he sees in the Chimaera
otherwise Bellerus, the monster slain by Bellerophon,
another version of Balar of the Evil Eye, the fire which
comes out of the Chimaera's throat, and the deadly
beam shot from Balar's evil eye, both, it seems probable, originally typifying the lightning.   But into
intricacies of mythology this is no place to ramble.

O'Donovan, indeed, thought that the de Dananns were a real race of men. So much of our oldest topographical nomenclature is connected with them, and so many still-remaining tumuli are ascribed to them, that he says, "these monuments are of the most remote antiquity, and prove that the Tuatha de Dananns were a real people, though their history is so much wrapped up in fable and obscurity," but he himself has given us the best of reasons for believing that they were not a real people, in this statement, "it seems very strange that our genealogists trace the pedigree of no family living for the last thousand years to any of the kings or chieftains of the Tuatha de Dananns, while several families of the Fir-Bolgic descent are mentioned in Hy-Many and other parts of Connacht."

CHAPTER VII.

THE RED BRANCH OR HEROIC CYCLE.

T HE mythological tales dealt with peoples, with dynasties, with, possibly, the struggle between good and evil principles; there is over it all a shadowy sense of vagueness, of vastness, of uncertainty. The heroic cycle, on the other hand, deals with the history of the Milesians themselves within a brief but well-defined period, and the romances relating to it are sharply drawn, numerous and ancient, many of them fine in both conception and execution. Here we seem for the first time to find ourselves upon historical ground. Cuchulain, Conor mac Nessa, Fergus mac Roy, Naesi and Déirdre, Mève, and Conall Cearnach have about them all the circumstantiality which is wanting to the dim, mist-magnified, and distorted forms of the mysterious Dagda, Nuada, Bres, Balar, Dana, and their fellows. Not that the mysterious is not ap-

parent in this cycle also. Cuchulain's birth, his courtship, to some extent his death, are mysterious enough, as is the metempsychosis of the souls which finally settled in the wondrous bulls which occasioned the great war, as is the sickness of the Ultonians, and much more. But these are excrescences no more affecting the conduct of the history than do the actions of the gods affect the war round Troy ; events' are sufficiently motivated upon reasonable human grounds, and there is a higher air of reality about' them. This is as it should be, for, according to the annalists, over seventeen hundred years had elapsed since the events recorded in the last cycle took place, and the characters who now make their appearance are about contemporaneous with the birth of Christ.*

Of this period, the great event is the long war between Connacht and Ulster, brought about by the murder of the sons of Usnach, a war which included the attempt of Mève, Queen of Connacht, to plunder Cuailgne in Louth. All the Irish world † knows the story of Déirdre, which gave rise to the great war— how Conor, King of Ulster, obeying a prophecy,

---

* The Tuatha de Danann had, according to the Four Masters, conquered Ireland Anno Mundi circiter 3303, and Eochaidh Feidhleach, the father of the great Mève, Queen of Connacht, came to the throne A.M. 5058. He died in 5069, *i.e.*, a little more than a hundred years before the birth of Christ.

† Yet when in Trinity College, a few years ago, the subject— the first Irish subject for twenty-seven years—set for the Vice-Chancellor's prize in English verse was " Déirdre," it was found that the students did not know what that word meant, or what Déirdre was, whether animal, vegetable, or mineral. So true it is that, despite all the efforts of Davis and his fellows, there are yet two nations in Ireland. Trinity College might to some extent bridge the gap if she would, but she has not even attempted it.

reared her in a solitary rath apart from all human beings, designing to make her his own wife when of age ; how the maiden became enamoured of Naesi, who fled with her to Alba, along with his two brothers ; how Conor lured them back again by Fergus mac Roy, who pledged them his word that no harm was intended for them ; how the king, having craftily separated Fergus from them, slew them, and the son of Fergus with them ; and how Fergus, in bitter indignation at his pledged word being broken, attacked and burned Conor's capital, Emania, and finally retired into Connacht, whence he kept up incessant incursions upon Ulster, with the aid of the Connacht warriors, for nearly ten years. The slaughter of the sons of Usnach and the melancholy death of Déirdre is one of the most pathetic tales of this cycle.

By far the greatest and most important of these romances, however, is that of Mève's excursion to carry off the bull of Cuailgne in Louth ; this is the well-known Táin Bo Cuailgne, or Cattle-spoiling of Cooley, and it is one which throws much light upon early Irish society and manners. Like most of the tales belonging to this cycle, it is eminently Pagan in tone and conception. Indeed, the heroic cycle had been pretty well crystallised into form by the seventh century, and the romances had by that time substantially assumed the shape in which we now find them.

This celebrated story opens with a conversation between Mève, Queen of Connacht, and Oilioll, her husband, which ends in a dispute as to which of them is the richest. There was no modern Married Woman's Property Act in force, but Irish women seem to have been at all times much more sympathetically treated by the Celtic tribes than by the harder and more stern races of Teutonic and northern blood, and Irish ladies seem to have been free to enjoy their own property and dowries. The story, then, begins with this dispute as to which, husband or wife, be the richer in this world's goods, and the argument at last becomes so heated that the pair decide to have all their possessions brought together to compare them one with the other, and judge by actual observation which is the most valuable. They collected accordingly, jewels, bracelets, metal, gold, silver, flocks, herds, ornaments, etc., and found that, in point of wealth, they were much the same, but that there was one great bull called the Finn-bheannach, or White-horned, who was really calved by one of Mève's cows, but being endowed with a certain amount of intelligence, considered it disgraceful to be under a woman, and so had gone over to Oilioll's herds. With him Mève had nothing that could compare. She made enquiry, however, and found out from her chief courier that there was in the district of Cuailgne, in Louth, (Mève lived at Cruachan, now Croghan, in Roscommon) a most celebrated bull called the Dun Bull of Cuailgne, belonging to a chieftain of the name of Darè. To him, accordingly, she sends an embassy, requesting the loan of the bull for one year, and promising fifty heifers in return. Darè was quite willing, and promised to lend the animal. He was, in fact, pleased, and treated the embassy generously, giving them good lodging and plenty of food and drink—too much drink, in fact. The fate of nations is said to often hang upon a thread. On this occasion that of Ulster and Connacht depended upon a drop more or less absorbed by one of the ten men who constituted Mève's embassy. This man took, unfortunately, a drop too much, and Darè's steward coming in at the moment, heard him say that it was small thanks to his master to give his bull, "For if he hadn't given it we'd have taken it." That word decided the fate of provinces. The steward, indignant at such an outrage, ran and told his master, and Darè swore that now he would send no bull, and swore too, but that the ten men were envoys he would have hanged them. With indignity they were dismissed, and returned empty-handed, to Mève's boundless indignation. She in her turn swore she would have the bull in spite of Darè. She immediately sent out to collect her armies, and invited Leinster and Munster to join her. She was, in fact, able to muster most of the three provinces to march against Ulster to take the bull from Darè, and in addition she had Fergus mac Roy and about 1,500 Ulster warriors who had never returned to their homes, nor forgiven Conor for the murder of the sons of Usnach. She crossed the Shannon at Athlone, and marched on to Kells, within a few miles of Ulster, and there she pitched her standing camp. She was accompanied by her husband and her daughter, who was the fairest among women. Her mother had secretly promised her hand to every leader in her army, in order to nerve them to greater feats of arms.

It so chanced that the territory upon whose border they were now encamped belonged to the great Cuchulain himself, at this time not much more than a youth, and it was within his patrimony that Darè lived, who was owner of the Dun Bull. Cuchulain alone stepped forth to meet the armies of Connacht, and endeavoured to delay them by challenging them to a series of single combats with himself, in which he was always victorious, until Mève tired of this, hurled her entire army upon Ulster, carried off the Dun Cow, and ravaged the country up to the gates of

Emania, Conor's capital, thereby fulfilling the prophecy of Déirdre :—

> Woe to Eman, roof and wall,
> Woe to the Red Branch, hearth and hall,
> Tenfold woe and black dishonour
> To the foul and false Clan Conor.

The most interesting incident in the romance is the single combat between Cuchulain and his old friend Ferdiad, who very much against his will was in spite of himself persuaded by Mève's importunities and promises, and also the hope of gaining her beautiful daughter, to fight his ancient comrade.

Here is a description of the conduct of the two warriors after their first day's fighting.

THE FIGHT AT THE FORD.

"They ceased fighting ;* they threw their weapons away from them into the hands of their charioteers. Each of them approached the other forthwith and each put his hand round the other's neck and gave him three kisses. Their horses were in the same paddock that night, and their charioteers at the same fire ; and their charioteers spread beds of green rushes for them with wounded men's pillows to them. The professors of healing and curing came to heal and cure them, and they applied herbs,

---

* I follow here for the most part the translation given by Sullivan in his addenda to O'Curry's *Manners and Customs*, but it is an exceedingly faulty and defective one, from an accurately linguistic point of view ; however, even if a few words are mistranslated or their sense mistaken, it is quite immaterial here. Windisch is said to have finished a complete translation of the Táin, but it has not yet appeared anywhere. See, however, Max Netlau's texts of the Ferdiad episode in vols. 10 and 11 of the *Revue Celtique*.

and plants of healing and curing, to their stabs and
their cuts and their gashes, and to all their wounds.
Of every herb and of every healing and curing plant
that was put to the stabs and cuts and gashes, and to
all the wounds of Cuchulain, he would send an equal
portion from him, westward over the Ford to Ferdiad,
so that the men of Erin might not be able to say,
should Ferdiad fall by him, that it was by better
means of cure that he was enabled to kill him.

" Of each kind of food and of palatable pleasant
intoxicating drink that was sent by the men of Erin to
Ferdiad, he would send a fair moiety over the ford
northwards to Cuchulain, because the purveyors of
Ferdiad were more numerous than the purveyors of
Cuchulain.   All the men of Erin were purveyors to
Ferdiad for beating off Cuchulain from them, but the
Bregians only were purveyors to Cuchulain, and they
used to come to converse with him at dusk every night.
They rested there that night."

The narrative goes on to describe the next day's
fighting which was carried on from their chariots " with
their great broad spears," and which left them both in
such evil plight that the professors of healing and
curing " would do nothing more for them, because of
the dangerous severity of their stabs and their cuts and
their gashes and their numerous wounds, than to apply
witchcraft and incantations and charms to them to
staunch their blood and their bleeding and their gory
wounds."   Their meeting on the next day follows.

" They arose early the next morning, and came forward to the field of battle. Cuchulain perceived an ill-
visaged and a greatly lowering cloud on Ferdiad that
day. 'Badly dost thou appear to-day, O Ferdiad,'
said Cuchulain, 'thy hair has become dark this day,
and thine eye has become drowsy, and thine own

form and features and appearance have departed from
thee.' 'It is not from fear or terror of thee that I am
so this day ;' said Ferdiad, 'for there is not in Erin
this day a champion that I could not subdue.' And
Cuchulain was complaining and bemoaning, and he
spake these words, and Ferdiad answered :

CUCHULAIN.

'Oh, Ferdiad is it thou
Wretched man thou art I trow,
By a guileful woman won
To hurt thine old companion.'

FERDIAD.

'Oh, Cuchulain, fierce of fight,
Man of wounds and man of might,
Fate constrains each one to stir
Moving towards his sepulchre.'" *

The lay is then given, each of the heroes reciting a
verse in turn, and it is very possibly upon these lays
that the prose narrative is built up. The third day's
fighting is then described in which the warriors used
their "heavy hard-smiting swords," or rather swords
that gave "blows of size." The story then continues:
"They cast away their weapons from them into the
hands of their charioteers, and though it had been the
meeting, pleasant and happy, griefless and spirited of
two men that morning, it was the separation, mournful,
sorrowful, dispirited of the two men that night.
"Their horses were not in the same enclosure that

---

* This is the metre of the original. The last lines are literally
" A man is constrained to come unto the sod where his final
grave shall be." The metre of the last line is wrong in the LL,
version of the original.

night. Their charioteers were not at the same fire. They rested that night there.

"Then Ferdiad arose early next morning, and went forward alone to the ford of battle, for he knew that that day would decide the battle and the fight, and he knew that one of them would fall on that day there, or that they both would fall.

. . . .

Ferdiad displayed many noble, wonderful, varied feats on high that day which he never learned with any other person, neither with Scathach, nor with Uathach nor with Aifè, but which were invented by himself that day against Cuchulain.

"Cuchulain came to the ford and he saw the noble, varied, wonderful, numerous feats which Ferdiad displays on high. 'I perceive there my friend Laeg' (said Cuchulain to his charioteer) 'the noble, varied, wonderful, numerous feats which Ferdiad displays on high, and all these feats will be tried on me in succession, and, therefore it is, that if it be I who shall begin to yield this day, thou art to excite, reproach, and speak evil to me, so that the ire of my rage and anger shall grow the more on me. If it be I who prevail, then thou shalt laud me, and encourage me, and speak good words to me, that my courage may be greater.'* 'It shall so be done indeed, O Cuchulain,' said Laeg.

"And it was then Cuchulain put his battle-suit of

---

* A common trait, even in modern Gaelic tales, as in the story of Illann. son of the King of Spain, where his sweetheart urges him to the battle by chanting his pedigree. and in Campbell's story of Conall Gulban, where the daughter of the King of Lochlann urges her bard to exhort her champion in the fight lest he be defeated, and to give him Brosnachadh file fir-ghlic, *i.e.,* the urging of a truly wise poet.

battle, and of combat, and of fight on him, and he displayed noble, varied, wonderful, numerous feats on high on that day, that he never learned from anybody else, neither with Scathach, nor with Uathach, nor with Aifè; Ferdiad saw those feats and he knew they would be plied against him in succession.

"'What weapons shall we resort to, O Ferdiad?' said Cuchulain. 'To thee belongs thy choice of weapons till night,' said Ferdiad.

"'Let us try the Ford Feat, then,' said Cuchulain.

"'Let us, indeed,' said Ferdiad. Although Ferdiad thus spoke his consent, it was a cause of grief to him to speak so, because he knew that Cuchulain was used to destroy every hero and every champion who contended with him in the Feat of the Ford.

"Great was the deed, now, that was performed on that day at the ford—the two heroes, the two warriors, the two champions of Western Europe, the two gift and present and stipend-bestowing hands of the north-west of the world, the two beloved pillars of the valour of the Gael, and the two keys of the bravery of the Gael, to be brought to fight from afar through the instigation and intermeddling of Ailill and Mève.

"Each of them began to shoot at other with their missive weapons from the dawn of early morning till the middle of midday. And when midday came the ire of the men waxed more furious, and each of them drew nearer to the other. And then it was that Cuchulain on one occasion sprang from the brink of the ford and came on the boss of the shield of Ferdiad son of Daman, for the purpose of striking his head over the rim of his shield from above. And it was then that Ferdiad gave the shield a blow of his left elbow and cast Cuchulain from him like a bird on the brink of the ford. Cuchulain sprang from the brink of the ford again till he came on the boss of the shield of Ferdiad son of Daman, for the purpose of striking his head over the rim of the shield from above. Ferdiad gave the shield a stroke of his left knee, and cast Cuchulain from him like a little child on the brink of the ford.

"Laeg [his charioteer] perceived that act. 'Alas, indeed,' said Laeg, 'the warrior who is against thee casts thee away as a lewd woman would cast her child. He throws thee as foam is thrown by the river. He grinds thee as a mill would grind fresh malt. He pierces thee as the felling axe would pierce the oak. He binds thee as the woodbine binds the tree. He darts on thee as the hawk darts on small birds, so that henceforth thou hast nor call, nor right, nor claim to valour or bravery to the end of time and life, thou little fairy phantom,' said Laeg.

"Then up sprang Cuchulain with the rapidity of the wind and with the readiness of the swallow, and with the fierceness of the dragon and the strength of the lion into the troubled clouds of the air the third time, and he alighted on the boss of the shield of Ferdiad son of Daman to endeavour to strike his head over the rim of his shield from above. And then it was the warrior gave the shield a shake, and cast Cuchulain from him into the middle of the ford, the same as if he had never been cast off at all.

"And it was then that Cuchulain's first distortion came on, and he was filled with swelling and great fulness, like breath in a bladder, until he became a terrible, fearful, many-coloured, wonderful Tuaig, and he became as big as a Fomor, or a man of the sea, the great and valiant champion, in perfect height over Ferdiad.*

* Compare this with the Berserker rage of the Northmen.

"So close was the fight they made now that their heads met above and their feet below and their arms in the middle over the rims and bosses of their shields. So close was the fight they made that they cleft and loosened their shields from their rims to their centres. So close was the fight which they made that they turned and bent and shivered their spears from their joints to their hafts! Such was the closeness of the fight which they made that the Bocanachs and Bananachs and wild people of the glens and demons of the air screamed from the rims of their shields, and from the hilts of their swords, and from the hafts of their spears. Such was the closeness of the fight which they made that they cast the river out of its bed and out of its course, so that it might have been a reclining and reposing couch for a king or for a queen in the middle of the ford, so that there was not a drop of water * in it unless it dropped into it by the trampling and the hewing which the two champions and the two heroes made in the middle of the ford. Such was the intensity of the fight which they made, that the stud of the Gaels darted away in fright and shyness, with fury and madness, breaking their chains and their yokes, their ropes and their traces, and that the women and youths and small people and camp-followers, and non-combatants of the men of Erin broke out of the camp southwestwards.

"They were at the edge-feat of swords during the time. And it was then that Ferdiad found an unguarded moment upon Cuchulain, and he gave him a stroke of the straight-edged sword, and buried it in his

---

* Cf. the common Gaelic folk-lore formula, "they would make soft of the hard and hard of the soft, and bring cold springs or fresh water out of the hard rock with their wrestling."

body until his blood fell into his girdle, until the ford
became reddened with the gore from the body of the
battle-warrior. Cuchulain could not endure this, for
Ferdiad continued his unguarded stout strokes, and his
quick strokes, and his tremendous great blows at him.
And he asked Laeg, son of Riangabhra, for the Gae
Bulg. The manner of that was this : it used to be set
down the stream and cast from between the toes [*lit.*,
in the cleft of the foot], it made the wound of one spear
in entering the body, but it had thirty barbs to open,
and could not be drawn out of a person's body until it
was cut out. And when Ferdiad heard the Gae Bulg
mentioned he made a stroke of the shield down to
protect his lower body. Cuchulain thrust the unerring
thorny spear off the centre of his palm over the rim of
the shield, and through the breast of the skin-protecting
armour, so that its further half was visible after pierc-
ing his heart in his body. Ferdiad gave a stroke of
his shield up to protect the upper part of his body,
though it was "the relief after the danger." The
servant set the Gae Bulg down the stream, and
Cuchulain caught it between the toes of his foot, and
he threw an unerring cast of it at Ferdiad till it passed
through the firm deep iron waistpiece of wrought iron,
and broke the great stone which was as large as a
mill-stone in three, and passed through the protections
of his body into him, so that every crevice and every
cavity of him was filled with its barbs.

" 'That is enough now, indeed,' said Ferdiad, 'I
fall of that. Now indeed may I say that I am sickly
after thee, and not by thy hand should I have fallen,'
and he said : [Here follow verses.]

. . . . . .

"Cuchulain ran towards him after that and clasped
his two arms about him, and lifted him with his arms

and his armour and his clothes across the ford north-ward, in order that the slain should be by the ford on the north, and not by the ford on the west, with the men of Erin.

"Cuchulain laid Ferdiad down there, and a trance and faint and weakness fell then on Cuchulain over Ferdiad. 'Good, O Cuchulain,' said Laeg, 'rise up now for the men of Erin are coming upon us, and it is not single combat they will give thee since Ferdiad, son of Daman, son of Darè has fallen by thee.'

"'Friend,' said he, 'what availeth me to arise after him that hath fallen by me?'"

The Conception of Conor, the Wooing of Emer, the Death of Conlaoch, Cuchulain's Rearing, Mac Datho's Swine, the Siege of Howth, the Intoxication of the Ultonians, Bricriu's Banquet, Emer's Jealousy and Cuchulain's Pining, the Death of the Children of Usnach, the Death of Cuchulain, the Red Rout of Conall Cearnach, are amongst the best-known tales belonging to this cycle.

G

CHAPTER VIII.

THE FENIAN CYCLE.

UCHULAIN'S life and love and death, entranced the ears of the great for many centuries; and into hundreds of bright eyes tears of pity had for a thousand years been conjured up by the pathetic tones of bards reciting the fate of her who perished for the sons of Usnach. The wars of Mève and Conor mac Nessa were household words in the hall of Muircheartach of the Leather Cloaks, and in the Palace at the Head of the Weir—Brian Boru's Kincora. Whosoever loved what was great in conception, and admired the broad sweep of the epic, called upon his bards to recite him the loves, the wars, the valour, and the deaths of the Red Branch Knights.* But there was yet another era consecrated in story-telling, another age of history, peopled by other characters, in which the households of many chief-tains, and no doubt many even of the chiefs them-selves delighted. This was the body of romances that were woven around Conn of the Hundred Battles, his son Art the Lonely, his grandson Cormac mac Art, and his great grandson Cairbre of the Liffey. This cycle of romance may be called the " Fenian " cycle, as dealing to some extent with Finn mac Cool and his Fenian†

* Moore's genius has stereotyped amongst us the term Red Branch Knight, which, however, has too much flavour of the mediæval about it. The Irish is *curadh*, "hero." The Irish for knight in the appellation White Knight, Knight of the Glen, etc., is Ridire (pronounced Rid-ĭr-yă, in Connacht often Rŭd-ĭr-yă) which is really a mediæval term, evidently borrowed from the German Ritter, *i.e.*, Rider. The Red Branch heroes never appear on horseback, but always in chariots.

† Moore helped to bring this word into common use under the form of Finnian in his melody : " The wine cup is circling in Alvin's Hall." It is probable that he derived the word from Finn, and meant by it "followers of Finn Mac Cool." The Irish word is Fiann (pronounced Fee-an) and has nothing to do with Finn Mac Cool. In the genitive it is na-Féine (na-Fayna). It is a noun of multitude, and means the Fenian body in general. The individual Fenian was called Féinnidhe, *i.e.*, a member of the Fenian force. The bands of militia were called Fianna (Feeăna). The English translation of Keating, made early in the last century by Dermod O'Connor, does not use the term " Fenian " at all, but translates it by " Irish Militia." Nor does O'Halloran, in 1778, when he published his history seem to have known the word. We find Miss Brooke, however, as early as 1796, using the term Fenian in the following lines :—

" He cursed in rage the Fenian chief,
And all the Fenian race."

militia, or the "Ossianic" cycle since Ossian, Finn's son, is supposed to have been the author of many of the poems which belong to it.

In point of time, as reckoned by the Irish annalists and historians, the men of the Fenian cycle lived something about 200 years later than those of the Cuchulain era,[*] and in none of the romances do we see even the faintest confusion or sign of intermingling the characters belonging to the different cycles. One of the surest proofs—if proof were needed—that Mac Pherson's brilliant "Ossian" had no Gaelic original, is the way in which the men and events of the two separate cycles are jumbled together.

As the war between Ulster and Connacht, which followed the death of the children of Usnach, is the great historic event which serves as basis to so many of the Red Branch romances, so the principal thread of history round which many of the Fenian stories group themselves, is the gradual and slowly-increasing enmity which proclaimed itself between the High Kings of Erin and their Fenian cohorts, resulting at last in the battle of Gowra, the fall of the High King, and the destruction of the Fenians.

Thus, in the Battle of Cnucha is related how Cool,[†] the father of Finn, made war upon Conn of the Hun-

And Halliday in his edition of Keating, published in 1808, also talks in a foot-note of "Fenian heroes." It was John O'Mahony, the Head-Centre, a brilliant Irish scholar, who first, by a happy inspiration, connected the I.R.B., or its equivalent, with the ancient Irish militia, and by calling them Fenians, perpetuated for all time an ancient historic memory.

[*] Cormac mac Art came to the throne A.D. 227, according to the Four Masters, A.D. 213 according to Keating.

[†] In Irish _Cúmhal_, but "mh" in the middle of a word is sounded as "v" or "w," hence the word is pronounced Coowal, or more shortly, Cool.

dred Battles because he had raised Crimhthan [Crivhan] of the Yellow Hair to the throne of Leinster, and how he obtained the aid of the Munster princes in the war. At the battle of Cnucha, or Castleknock, near Cool's rath,—now Rathcoole, some ten miles from Dublin,— Cool was routed and slain by the celebrated Connacht champion, Aedh mac Morna, who lost an eye in the battle and was thenceforth called Goll (or the blind)* mac Morna. Many of the Munster Fenians followed Cool in this battle, and we find here the broadening rift between the Fenians of Munster and of Connacht, which ultimately tended to bring about the dissolution of the whole body.

Again we find in the fine tale called the Battle of Moy Muchruime, how Finn, through spite at his father Cool being thus killed by Conn of the Hundred Battles, kept out of the way when Conn's son Art was fighting the great battle of Moy Muchruime, and gave him no assistance.

And again it was partly because Finn kept out of the way on that occasion that Conn's great grandson fought the battle of Gowra against Finn's son Ossian, and his grandson Oscar, a battle which put an end to Fenian power for ever.

Of many of these tales we find two redactions, that of the old vellum MSS. and that of the modern paper ones, the latter being as a rule much more lengthy and decorative. I suspect, however, that in most cases only condensed versions of romances were committed to the most ancient books, writing being then less common, and vellum rarer and more expensive, and that the bards whose business it was to recite them,

---

* The word is long obsolete. Goll is a stock character in Fenian folk-lore.

lengthened and adorned them for themselves while in the act of oral delivery. Here, for instance, is a specimen of a passage written at full length in the more modern paper books, but slurred over or wholly disregarded in the old vellum ones; it is the sailing of Cool, Finn's father, to Ireland, to take the throne of Leinster. I translate this from a modern manuscript of the battle of Cnucha in my own possession, as a good instance of the decorative and in places inflated style of the later redactions of many of the Fenian sagas.

The Sailing of Cool.

"Now the place where Cool chanced to be at that time was between the islands of Alba and the deserts of Fionn-Lochlan, for he was hunting and deer-stalking there. And the number of those who were with the overthrowing hero, Cool, in that place, was thrice fifty champions of his own near men; and he heard at that time that his country was left without any good king to defend it, and that Cauheer More* [King of Leinster] had fallen on the field of battle, and that there was no hero to keep the country. Thereupon those chieftains were of a mind to proceed unto the isolated green isle of Erin, there to maintain with valour and might the red-hand province of Leinster. And joyfully proceeded they straight forwards towards their ship.

"And there they quickly and expeditiously launched the towering wide-wombed broad-sailed bark, the freighted full-wide fair-broad firm-roped vessel, and they grasped their shapely well-formed broad-bladed well-prepared oars, and they made a powerful sea-

---

* In Irish Cáthaoir Mór.

great dashing dry-quick rowing over the broad hollow-deep full-foamed pools [of the sea], and over the rash-billowed vehement hollow-broken rollers, so that they shot their shapely ship under the junt house of each fair rock, in the shallows, nigh to the rough-bordered margin of the Eastern lands, over the smooth-less great-foaming lively-waved arms of the sea, so that each fierce, broad, constant foaming, bright-spotted, white-broken drop that the heroes left upon the sea-pool with that rapid rowing formed [themselves] like great torrents upon soft mountains.

"When that valiant powerful company perceived the moaning of the loud billowy waves, and the breaking forth of the ocean from her barriers, and the swelling of the abyss from her places, and the loud convulsion of the sea from her smooth streams, it was then they hoisted the variegated tough-cordaged sharp-pointed mast in the centre of the galley narrow-cornered and broad-bosomed, and they raised aloft their fair greatly-shining well-answering truly-wrought quick-cordaged sail, upon the mast with much speed. And when the great foundation-blasts of the angry wind touched the even upright-standing, sword-straight masts, and when the huge-flying, loud-voiced, broad-bordered sails swallowed the wind attacking them suddenly with sharp voice, that stout, strong, active, powerful crew rose up promptly and quickly, and everyone went straight to his work with speed and promptitude, and they stretched forth their ready, courageous, white-coloured, brown-nailed hands most valiantly to the tackling, till they let the wind in loud sharp fast voice-bursts into the shrouds of the mast, so that the ship gave an eager, very quick, vigorous leap forward, right straight into the salt-ocean, till they arrived in the delightfully-clear, cold-pooled, plaintive-whistling, joy-

fully-calling reaches of the sea, and the dark sea rose
speedily around them in desperate, daring, flood-
ful *doisleana*, in commingling ridges, and in rough-
grey, proud-tongued, gloomy-grim, blue-capacious
valleys, and in impetuous showers-topped wombs (of
water) ; and the great merriment of the cold wind was
answered by the chieftains, strong-workingly, stout-
enduringly, truly-powerfully, and they proceeded to
manage and attend the high-ocean, until at last the
strong and powerful sea overcame the intention of the
high wind, and the murmur and giddy voice of the
deep was humbled by that great rowing, till the sea
became restful, smooth, and very calm behind them,
until they took port and harbour at Inver-Cholpa,
which is at this time called Drogheda."

Even those stories in which little or no mention is
made of the Fenians, as the Battle of Moy Léana,
between Conn of the Hundred Battles and Owen More,
in which Conn won for himself the sovereignty of the
whole island, and slew his rival, may be included in
this so called "Fenian" cycle, as well as such completely fabulous tales as Cormac mac Art's Branch,
and the like, because they deal with the same era and
the same characters.

The Fenian tales and poems are extraordinarily
numerous, and their conception and characteristics
are, in general, quite different from those relating to
the Red Branch. They have not the same wide
sweep, the same vastness and stature, the same weird-
ness, as the older cycle. They are more modern in
conception and surroundings ; there is no mention of
the war chariot which is so important a factor in the
older cycle, or if it is mentioned it plays no part. The
Fenians fight on foot or horseback, and in their saga-
cycle we meet mention of helmets and sometimes of

luireachs or mail-coats. Things are on a smaller scale, and exaggeration does not run all through the stories, but is confined to parts, and is set off by much of what is trivial and humorous. As the Táin Bo Chuailgne is the greatest tale in the first cycle, so the pursuit of Diarmuid and Gráinne* is perhaps the best executed of those in the second, but even it is defaced by several exaggerated incidents which have little or no bearing on the story. The lengthy piece called the Dialogue of the Ancients contained in the *Book of Lismore* is, from a social and topographical point of view, the most valuable.

The Fenian tales became in later times the distinctly popular ones. They were far more of the people and for the people than those of the Red Branch. They were most intimately bound up with the life and thought and feelings of the whole Gaelic race, high and low, both in Ireland and Scotland, and the development of Fenian Saga, for a period of one thousand two hundred or one thousand five hundred years, is one of the most remarkable examples in the world of continuous literary evolution. I use the word evolution advisedly, for there was probably not a century from the seventh to the eighteenth in which new stories, poems, and redactions of sagas concerning Finn and the Fenians were not invented and put in circulation, while to this very day many

---

* Pronounced Graan-ya. This story has had the good fortune to have been edited twice in Irish and English, and also translated into English by Dr. Joyce, who, however, omits the cynical but very characteristic conclusion. This story was only known to exist in quite modern MSS. but I recently discovered a fine copy written about the year 1660, among Dr. Reeve's MSS. about half of which were secured the other day by the Royal Irish Academy.

stories never committed to manuscript are current
about them amongst the Irish and Scotch Gaelic-
speaking populations.   We have found no such steady
interest evinced by the people in the Red Branch
romances, and in attempting to collect Irish folk-lore
I have found next to nothing about Cuchulain and
his contemporaries, but vast quantities about Finn,
Ossian, Oscar, Goll, and Conan.   The one cycle,
antique in tone, language, and surroundings, was
that of the chiefs, the great men, and the bards, the
other—at least in later times—more that of the un-
bardic classes and of the people.

I do not mean to say that many of the Cuchulain
stories were not copied into modern MSS. and circu-
lated freely among the people all over Ireland during
the eighteenth century and the beginning of this, especially Cuchulain's training, Conlaoch's (his son's)
death, the Fight at the Ford, and others ; but these
appear never to have put out shoots and blossoms
from themselves, and to have generated new and yet
again new stories, as did the ever-youthful Fenian
tales ; nor do they appear to have equally entwined
themselves at this day round the popular imagination.

A striking instance of how the Ossianic tale continued to develop down to the eighteenth century
was supplied me the other day when examining the
Reeves collection.   I there came upon a story in
a Louth MS., written, I think, in the last century,
which seemed to me to contain one of the latest
developments of Ossianic saga.   It is called The
Adventures of Dubh mac Deaghla [D'yala] and it tells
of how a prophet was born of the race of Eireamhóin,
"and all say," adds the writer, "that it was he was the
Druid who prophesied to Fiacha Sreabhtuinne (Srav-

tinna) that he would fall in the battle of Dubh-Cumair by the three brothers Caireall, Muircach, and Aedh."* He also "prophesied to the race of Toole that Cairbrè of the Liffey was that far branching tree which was to spread round about through the great circuit of Erin, around which smote the powerful wind from the south-west, overthrowing it wholly to the ground—which wind meant the Fenians, as had been announced by the smith's daughter." † The Fenians, it seems, heard that Torna had prophesied about them, and intended to kill him ; and he and his family had to emigrate to Britain. From this he sends a letter, in true epistolatory style, to an old friend of his, one Conor, son of Dathach, beginning "dear friend"—an evident mark I think of seventeenth, or possibly eighteenth century authorship, for there are no letters, so far as I know, written in this style in the older literature, and this piece evidently follows a Latin or a Spanish, or pos-

---

* These MSS., 54 volumes in number, had belonged to Mr. MacAdam, Editor of the *Ulster Journal of Archæology*, from whom Bishop Reeves bought them for £100. Many of them had before that belonged to O'Reilly, the lexicographer, and some of them are mentioned in Whitelaw and Walsh's *History of Dublin* as then existing in the city. On the lamented death of that great scholar they were put up to auction, when the Royal Irish Academy bought 32 of the volumes, the rest being unfortunately scattered again to the four winds of heaven. For his exertions and generosity in securing even so many of these MSS., especially those which at first sight looked least important, but which contained treasures of folk-lore and folk-song, the Hon. Treasurer, Rev. Maxwell Close, has placed Irish-speaking Ireland under yet another debt of gratitude to him. It is not always that which is most ancient which is also most valuable from either a literary or a national stand-point, nor is a manuscript necessarily valueless because it has no philological importance.

† This is in allusion to the romance of Moy Muchruime, where we read of the prophecy and what followed.

sibly even an English model. However this may be, Torna's letter asks Conor for news of the situation, and in time receives the following answer :—

THE LETTER.

" To Torna son of Dubh, our dear
friend in Glen Fuinnse in Britain
in Saxony.

" Thy affectionate missive was read by me as soon as it arrived and it had been a cause of joy to me, were it not for the way we are at Tara at this moment.

" For we never felt until the Munster Fenians came and encamped at the marsh of Old Raphoe and Treibhe to the south-west. The warriors of Leinster also and *Baoisgnidh*, together with Clan Ditribh and Clan Boirchne, were to the south of them, towards the bottom of the stream of Gowra, and on the west towards the old fort of Mève ; and that same evening the king, having received an account of the encamping of the Fenians, urges messengers secretly to Connacht, to the clan of Conal Cruachna, that they might come, along with all the king's friends from the western border of Erin. And other messengers he despatches to Scotland for the clan of Garaidh Glúnmhar, desiring Oscar of the blue javelin, Aedh, Argal, and Airtre to come from abroad without delay, and that secretly.

" On the early morning of the morrow, before the stars of the air retired, the king urged the Druids of Tara against the Fenians, to argue with them, and ask what was the cause of their rebelling in this guise, of who it was with whom they had now come to do battle, because they appeared not in habiliments of peace or friendship, but a blush of anger appeared in the face and countenance of every several man of them.

" 'And there is another unlawful thing of which ye are guilty,' said the Druids, 'which shows that ye have broken the vow of allegiance and obedience to your king, in that ye have come in array and garb of battle to the door of his fortress without receiving his leave or advice, without giving him notice or warning. To what art [point of the compass] do ye travel, or on what have ye set your mind [that ye act not] as is the right and due of a prince's subjects, and as was always before this the habitude of the bands that came before ye, and as it shall be with honest people till the end of the world ! '

" However, now, the druids are a-preaching to them and casting at them bold storm-showers of reproofs, by way of retarding them till the coming back of the messengers who went abroad, for the son of Cool is not amongst them to excite them against us ; and we hope that they will remain thus until help come to us. For this is the eleventh day since the Druids went from us, and our watchmen, who observe what approaches and what departs, disclose all tidings to us, and they are ever a-listening to the loud argument of the Druids and the captains against one another. Moreover, the desire of the Fenians to make a rapid assault upon Tara is the less from their having heard that Cairbrè was gone on his royal round to Dún Sreabhtainne to visit Fiacha,* though he is really not gone there, but to a certain

---

* Fiacha was the king's son, and succeeded him in the sovereignty. He was finally slain by his nephews, the celebrated Three Collas—they who afterwards burned Emania and caused the sun of the Ultonian dynasty and the Red Branch knights, after blazing in splendour for over 700 years, to set in blood and flame, never to rise again.

place under cover of night with his women and the
royal jewels of Tara.   And it was lucky for him that
he did not go to Dún Sreabhtainne, for the Fenians
had sent Coirioll, and nine mighty men with him, to
plunder Dún Sreabhtainne.   In that, however, they
miscarried, for Fiacha's tutor was gone off before
that with his pupil, by order of the king, to the same
place where the women were.   That, however, we
shall pursue no further at present.

"But it is easy for you, who are knowledgeable, to form
a judgment upon the state in which the inhabitants of
a country must be, over which a whelming calamity is
about to fall.   Let me leave off.   And here we send
our affectionate greeting to you, and to ye all, with the
hope of some time seeing you in full health, but I have
small hope of it.

> " From your faithful friend till death, Conor,
> son of Dathach, in Tara, the royal fortress
> of Erin.   Written the 20th day of the month
> of March, in the year of the age of the world
> * * * *" [the figures in the MS. are not
> clear, and I cannot read them].

The romance, which is a long one, is chiefly occu-
pied with the events relating to the family of Dubh
mac Deaghla in Britain. But later on in the book the
Conor who despatched this letter turns up, and gives
in person a most vivid description of the battle of
Gowra, and the events which followed his letter.

I have only instanced and quoted from this comparatively unimportant story as showing one of the
very latest developments of Fenian literature, and as
proving how thoroughly even the seventeenth and
eighteenth century Gaels realized and were impreg-

nated with the spirit of the Fenian cycle, and also as a peculiar specimen of what rarely happens in literature, but is always of great interest when it does happen— a specimen of unconscious saga developing into semi-conscious romance.

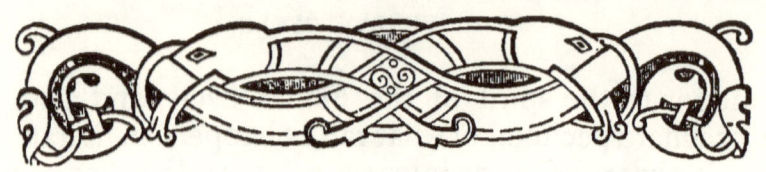

CHAPTER IX.

WHO WERE THE FENIANS?

THE vigorous strides made of late in the study of comparative folk-lore has awakened renewed interest in the question who or what were the Fenians; and so much has been lately said and written about this that I cannot afford, even in this light sketch of Gaelicl iterature, to pass it by, even though the inquiry prove a dry one. Those who think it so may skip this chapter.

The question we are now confronted with is this: May not the principal characters of the Cuchulain and Ossianic saga cycles, so far from being real historical personages, never have existed at all; may they not be either creatures of the imagination, or else may not the stories about them be ancient mythological tales of tribe gods, who are here euhemerized that is represented as men?

This question is not yet satisfactorily set at rest and may never be.

Of course all the Irish annalists and historians from Tighearnach, who died A.D. 1088, down to the Four Masters and Keating, and from that down to Eugene O'Curry, accepted unhesitatingly the genuine historical character of these sagas, and believed in the accounts handed down of the cause and date of Finn's death. The but-slightly-critical Keating, sensible even in his day, that objections as to the historical character of Finn and his contemporaries might be raised, goes out of his way—which he does not do for Cuchulain, probably regarding his historical character as above suspicion—to make these rationalistic remarks. "Now I hold it untrue," he says, "for any person to assert that Finn and the Fenians never had existence. For in testimony of their having really existed we have still remaining the three sorts of proof whereby all historical facts whatsoever are tried, except those recorded in Holy Writ. These are, firstly common oral tradition handed down from father to son ; secondly, ancient written documents ; and thirdly, ancient landmarks and monumental remains. We have ever heard and are constantly hearing it repeated from mouth to mouth that Finn and the Fenians once had existence, and again our ancient books record their adventures very fully, and we still have living witnesses of their existence in the ancient names attached to the localities and monumental remains called after them, as Finn's Seat upon Slievenamon, called after Finn o Baoisgne, Glen Garaidh, called after Garaidh Black-knee, son of Mórna, which lies in Ui Fathaidh, and Diarmuid and Gráinne's Bed in Ui

H

Fiacrach Aidhnè, now called O'Shaughnessy's Country, and so likewise of numbers of other localities throughout Ireland.

"But if any person should say that a great deal of what has been told about the Fenians is incredible, in that I hold him to be perfectly correct. But there was no country where men did not write untrue stories in the days of Paganism. I could even point out many stories of that kind, such as the 'Knight of the Sun,' * and similar ones, that were composed even in the times of the Faith, though there is no country where true and credible histories were not written at the same time. And thus though many fabulous and romantic tales such as the Battle of Ventry, the Fort of the Quicken Tree, the Flight of the Giolla Deachar and such like, have been written upon Finn and the Fenians for pastime's sake, it is certain that many true and credible histories have been written of them also."

After this Keating gives a full description of the Fenians, and asserts that they were nothing more than a standing militia maintained by the Irish kings, and not remarkable for size or stature.

O'Curry following Keating, says of Finn, "much that has been narrated of his exploits is no doubt apocryphal enough, but Finn himself is an undoubtedly historical character, and that he existed about the time at which his appearance is recorded in the annals, is as certain as that Julius Cæsar lived and ruled at the time stated on the authority of the Roman historians." "Das," mildly comments the ever-courteous Windisch, "ist zu viel gesagt"—"that is going a little too far." He himself, however, has written, "the Church adopted towards Pagan sagas the same

---

* I do not remember ever meeting this romance.

position that it did towards Pagan law. . . . I see then no sufficient ground for doubting that really genuine pictures of a pre-Christian culture are preserved to us in the individual sagas, pictures which of course are in some places blurred, and in others painted over by a different hand," and again commenting upon the way in which some of the Finn stories seem in their facts and colouring dependent upon the Cuchulain ones, he says, "of course it in no way follows from this that Finn was not an historical personage and never lived." And again on the voyage of the Sons of Usnach, he remarks, "the saga originated in Pagan and was pro-pagated in Christian times, and that, too, without its seeking fresh nutriment, as a rule, from Christian elements. But we must ascribe it to the influence of Christianity that what is specifically Pagan in Irish saga is blurred over and forced into the background. And yet there exist many whose contents are plainly mythological. The Christian monks were certainly *not the first* who reduced the ancient sagas to fixed form, but later on they copied them faithfully, and pro-pagated them, after Ireland had been converted to Christianity." * Zimmer, too, who stands side by side with Windisch ahead of all others amongst the Celtic scholars of Germany, has spoken thus in his *Keltische Studien,*† "Nothing," he says, "except a spurious criticism which takes for original and primitive the most palpable nonsense of which middle Irish writers of the twelfth and sixteenth centuries are guilty with regard to their own antiquity which is in many respects strange and foreign to them—nothing but such a criticism can on the other hand make the attempt to

* Windisch, *Irische Texte*, I., pp. 61, 62, 151 and 253.
† II. Heft, p. 159.

doubt of the historical character of the chief persons
of the saga cycles. For we believe Medbh, Conchobar
mac Nessa, Cuchulain, and Finn mac Cumhail are
exactly as much historical personalities as Arminius
or Dietrich of Bern, or Etzel, and their date is just as
well determined as that of the above mentioned heroes
and kings who are glorified in song by the Germans,
even though in the case of Irish heroes and kings
external witnesses are wanting." M. Jubainville again,
who amongst French Celticists is *the master of those
who know*, and who has done more than all other men
to popularise Celtic studies, expresses himself thus :—
"We have no reason to doubt of the reality of the
persons who play the principal rôle in this cycle (of
Cuchulain);"* and of the story of the Boru tribute,
which took place about the year 90, he says again :—
"Le récit a pour base des faits réels, quoique certains
détails aient été créés par l'imagination." Last year,
it is true, Zimmer developed a theory that Finn was
really a Norseman, and that the Fenian cycle is in fact
posterior to the Norse invasion, but this paradoxical
theory has broken down, or at least has carried with
it none of the other great Celtic savants. Mr. Alfred
Nutt, on the other hand, has come to the conclusion, in his learned and interesting essay on the
Development of the Fenian Saga, appended to the
Gaelic Folk and Hero Tales collected by MacInnes,
that the whole groundwork of the Ossianic tales is
mythical. "Every Celtic tribe," says Mr. Nutt,
"possessed traditions both mythical and historical,
the former of substantially the same character, the
latter necessarily varying. Myth and history acted
and reacted upon each other, and produced heroic

* *Introduction à l'étude de la Littérature Celtique*, p. 287.

saga, which may be defined as myth tinged and distorted by history. The largest element is as a rule suggested by myth, so that the varying heroic sagas of the various portions of a race have always a great deal in common. These heroic sagas, together with the official or semi-official mythologies of the pre-Christian Irish are the subject-matter of the annals. They were thrown into a purely artificial chronological shape by men familiar with Biblical and classic history. A framework was thus created into which the entire mass of native legend was gradually fitted, whilst the genealogies of the race were modelled, or it may be remodelled in accord with it. In studying the Irish sagas, we may banish entirely from our mind all questions as to the "truth of the early portions of the annals. The subject-matter of the latter is mainly mythical, the mode in which it has been treated is literary. What residuum of historic truth may still survive can be but infinitesimal." According to this theory of Mr. Nutt's, both the Cuchulain and the Ossianic sagas were originally nothing but tribal myths, and probably myths belonging to different Gaelic tribes.* The deities of which they treated became in process of time euhemerised or regarded as real men, not deities, and in addition to this the legends were probably mixed up eventually with the exploits of some real men living in Ireland, and so the matter for innumerable tales, extending in their genesis and growth for over a period of a thousand years, was prepared. There is yet another hypothesis of which Dr. Skene

* My friend Mr. Larminie, who seems to have adopted this theory, ascribes the universally-known ever popular Fenian stories to the original inhabitants of Ireland and Scotland, and the cycle of the Red Branch to the dominant Aryan-speaking race, a most luminous suggestion if Mr. Nutt's theory be true. See his *West of Ireland Folk-tales.*

and Mr. Mac Ritchie, and perhaps the great folk-lorist, Iain Campbell of Islay, were champions—that the Fenians were a non-Celtic race of men, allied to or identical with the Picts of history.

The actual data that we have to go upon in estimating the genesis and development of the Fenian tales have been lucidly collected by Mr. Nutt. They are, as far as is known at present, as follows :—Gilla Caemhain the poet, who died in 1072, says that it was fifty-seven years after the battle of Moy Muchruime that Finn was treacherously killed " by the spear-points of Uirgriu's three sons." This would make Finn's death take place in 252, for Moy Muchruime was fought, according to the Four Masters, in A.D. 195. Tigearnach, the annalist, who died in 1088, writes that Finn was killed in A.D. 283 "by Aichleach, son of Duibhdrean, and the sons of Uirgriu, of the Luaighni of Tara, at Ath-Brea upon the Boyne." The poet Cinaeth O'Hartagain, who died in A.D. 985, wrote—"By the Fiann of Luagne was the death of Finn at Ath-Brea upon the Boyne." All these men in the tenth and eleventh centuries certainly believed Finn to have been a real man.

The two oldest miscellaneous Irish MSS. which we have are the Leabhar na h-Uidhre and the *Book of Leinster*. The Leabhar na h-Uidhre was compiled from older MSS. towards the close of the eleventh century, and the *Book of Leinster* some fifty years later. What then do we find in these MSS. about Finn and the Fenians? The oldest of them contains a copy of the famous poem of the bard Dallan Forgaill in praise of St. Columkille, which was so ancient in the middle of the eleventh century that it required to be glossed. In this gloss made, perhaps, in the eleventh century, but very possibly long before, there is a poem on winter ascribed to Finn, grandson of Baoisgne, that is our Finn mac Cool, and in the same commentary we find an explanation of the words " diu "= long, and " derc "=eye, in proof of which this verse is quoted, " As Gráinne," says the commentator " daughter of Cormac, said to Finn,

" There lives a man
On whom I would love to gaze long
For whom I would give the whole world,
All, all, though it is a delusion."

This verse quoted as containing two words which required explanation in or before the eleventh century, pre-supposes the story of Diarmuid and Gráinne. In addition to this we have in the same manuscript the apparently historical story of the " Cause of the Battle of Cnucha." We have also the story of Mongan, an Ulster King of the seventh century, according to the annalists, who declared that he was not what men took him to be, the son of the mortal Fiachna, but of the god, Manannán Mac Lir, and a re-incarnation of the great Finn, and calls back from the grave the famous Fenian Caoilte to prove it. This account is strongly relied upon by Mr. Nutt, to prove the wild mythological nature of the Finn story, but it is by no means unique in Irish literature, for we find the celebrated Tuan mac Cairrill had a second birth also, and the great Cuchulain too has his parentage ascribed to the god Lugha, not to Sualtam, his reputed father. Supposing Finn to have been a real historical character of the third century, there would be nothing absolutely extraordinary in the story arising in half-Pagan times that Mongan, also an historical character, was a re-incarnation of Finn.[*]

* It is, however, certainly curious that Cinaeth O'Hartagain,

In the second oldest miscellaneous manuscript, the *Book of Leinster*, the references to Finn and the Fenians are much more numerous, containing three poems ascribed to Ossian, Finn's son, five poems ascribed to Finn himself, two poems ascribed to Caoilte the Fenian poet, a poem ascribed to one of Finn's followers, allusions to Finn in a poem by one Gilla in Chomded, and in a poem by another bard, passages about Finn from the Dindsenchas or topographical tract, the account of the Battle of Cnámhross, in which Finn helps the Leinstermen against King Cairbre, the genealogy of Finn, and the genealogy of Diarmuid O Duibhne.

Again in the "Glossary" ascribed, and probably

who died A.D. 985, should have mentioned the name Mongan just before his lines on Finn.

> Mongan a diadem of all generations
> Fell by the Fiann of Kintyre,
> By the Fiann of Luagne was the death of Finn,
> At Ath-Brea on the Boyne.

Mongan, according to the eleventh century MS., was the contemporary of Dallan Forgaill, who died about the year 600, while Mongan, the Ulster King, was slain in 622. There is no real discrepancy in all this, and up to this point the annalistic scheme hangs fairly well together; but there is, says Mr. Nutt, one passage in the twelfth century Book of Leinster, which shows extraordinary disregard of all historical notions by making Finn interview St. Moling about the Boru tribute. There is, however, even here no historical confusion, for so far from calling him St. Moling, he is described as one of three foster brothers of Finn, and called Moling the Swift. The whole passage, however, is a clumsy invention, for first Finn sees a vision of angels that are to come, and afterwards another warrior sees a vision of priests saying Mass on the spot where they were then assembled, and Moling himself among the number. The whole passage is one of those ill-blending patched-up Christian passages by the tacking on of which to themselves, the Pagan stories received their permit from the Church.

truly, to Cormac, King-Bishop of Cashel, A.D. 837-903, there are two allusions to Finn, one of which refers to the unfaithfulness of his wife. This, indeed, is not contained in the oldest copy, but Whitley Stokes, than whom there can be no better authority, believes these allusions to belong to the older portion of the Glossary, a work which is probably much interpolated.

But, there is yet another proof of the antiquity of the Finn stories which Mr. Nutt does not note, and in some respects it is the most important and conclusive of all. For if, as D'Arbois de Jubainville has I think proved, the list of one hundred and eighty-seven historic tales contained in the *Book of Leinster*, was really drawn up at the end of the seventh or beginning of the eighth century, we find that even then Finn or his contemporaries were the subjects of or figure in several of them, as in the story of the Courtship of Ailbhe, daughter of King Cormac mac Art, by Finn; the Battle of Moy Much-ruime, where King Art, Cormac's father, was slain; the Cave of Bin Édair, where Diarmuid and Gráinne took shelter when pursued by Finn; the Adventures of Finn in Derc Fearna (the Cave of Dunmore) a lost tale; the Elopement of Gráinne with Diarmuid, and perhaps one or two more.

Thus, Finn is sandwiched in as a real person along with his other contemporaries, not only in tenth and eleventh century annalists and poets, but is also made the hero of historic romances as early as the seventh or eighth century. Side by side in our seventh–eight century list with the battle of Moy Mu-chruime, we find the battle of Moy Rath. We have both stories at full length, still preserved to us; both are couched in the same sort of language and coloured with the same literary pigments. The last, the battle of Moy Rath, we *know* to be historical; it can be proved; why should not the first be also? It is true that the one took place four hundred and thirty-eight years before the other, but the treatment of both is absolutely identical, and it is the merest accident that we happen to have external evidence for the latter and not for the former. If Finn is to be regarded as a myth, as a deity euhemerized, then must not Conn of the Hundred Battles and Eóghan [Owen] Mór, and all the rest go too? And yet Conn and Owen seem to have had an objective existence, since it was their struggle for supremacy in the second century which divided Ireland into the universally known divisions called Conn's half and Owen's half, whose bards wrote against each other so late as the year 1600, their lays on that occasion being collected in the celebrated book of poems, called the " Contention of the Bards." In other words I do not see anything to differentiate the case of Finn from that of the kings and heroes who were also the subjects of bardic stories, and whose deaths are recorded in the annals, except the accident that the creative imagination of the later Gaels happened to seize upon him, and make him and his contemporaries the nucleus of a vast litera-ture, instead of some other earlier or later group of, perhaps, equally deserving warriors. Finn has now become to all ears a pan-Gaelic champion just as Arthur became a Brythonic one.

CHAPTER X.

MISCELLANEOUS SAGAS.

ESIDES the three cycles of stories of which I have spoken, there exist a large number of independent sagas, dealing, some with pre-Christian events, others with events of the early middle ages. Out of the hundred and eighty-seven stories whose names are recorded in the *Book of Leinster*, about 120 seem to have utterly vanished ; of the others, many of which, however, are preserved only in the baldest and most condensed form, some four or five relate to the Fenian cycle, some eighteen to the Cuchulain stories, some eight or nine—mostly preserved in the brief and colourless digests of the *Book of Invasions*—are mythological, and about twenty-one are miscellaneous. Some of these latter are of the highest interest, antiquity, and importance. Of these, the Storming of the Bruidhean (Breean) or Court of Da Derga, is, if not the best conceived, yet as far as its text goes, the oldest and most important saga we have, with the exception of the Táin Bo Chuailgne. These two stories, substantially dating from the seventh century, and perhaps formed into shape long before that time, are preserved in the oldest miscellaneous MSS. which we possess, and throw more light upon Pagan manners, customs, and institutions, than perhaps any other.*

As for the period in which the story of the Court of Da Derga is laid, it is about coincident with that of the Red Branch cycle, only it does not deal with Emania and the Red Branch, but with Leinster, Tara, and the High King of Erin there resident. The High King at this time was Conairé the "Great," rightly so-called, if we may believe our Annals, for he had been a just, magnanimous, and, above all, fortunate ruler of all Ireland for fifty years.† So just was

---

* There is an almost complete copy of this saga in the Leabhar na-h-Uidhre, a MS. of about the year 1100. Like the Táin Bo Chuailgne, it has never been published even in a translation. The language is even harder and more archaic than that of the Táin. I have principally drawn upon O'Curry's description of it, for I confess that I can only guess at the meaning of a great part of the original. Were all Europe searched, the scholars who could give an adequate translation of it might be counted on the fingers of both hands—if not of one.

† According to the Four Masters, he was slain in A.M. 5161 [i e., 38 B.C.], after a reign of 70 years. "It was in the reign of Conairé," the Four Masters add, "that the Boyne annually cast its produce ashore at Inver Colpa. Great abundance of nuts were annually found upon the Boyne and the Buais. The cattle were without keeping in Ireland in his reign, on account of the greatness of the peace and concord. His reign was not thunder-

he and so strict, that he had sent into banishment
a number of lawless and unworthy persons who had
troubled his kingdom. Among these were his own
five foster brothers, whom he was reluctantly compelled to send into exile along with the others. These
people all turned to piracy, and plundered the coasts
of England, Scotland, and even Ireland, whenever they
found an opportunity of making a successful raid upon
the unarmed inhabitants. It so happened that the
son of the King of Britain, one Ingcel, also of Irish
extraction, had been banished by his father for his
crimes, and was now making his living in much the
same way as the predatory Irishmen. These two
parties having met, being drawn together by a fellow-
feeling and their common lawlessness, struck up a
friendship and made a league with one another. thus
doubling the strength of each. Soon after this the High
King found himself in the south, called thither to
settle, according to his wont, some dispute between
two rival chiefs. His business ended, he was leisurely
taking his way, with his retinue, back again to his
royal seat, when on entering the borders of Meath
he beheld the whole country towards Tara a sheet
of flame and rolling smoke. Terrified at this, and
divining that the banished pirates had made a descent in his absence, he turned aside and took the
great road that, leading from Tara to Dublin, passed
thence into the heart of Leinster. Pursuing this road,
the King crossed the Liffey in safety, and made for
the Bruighean (Bree-an), or Court of Da Derga, on

producing or stormy. It was little but the trees bent under the
greatness of their fruit." This notion of connecting good seasons
with good rulers was very common in Ireland. We find traces
of it as late as the sixteenth century.

the road close to the river Dothar or Dodder, called ever since, "Boher-na-breena,"* the "road of the court," close to Tallacht, not far from Dublin. This was one of the six great courts of universal hospitality in Erin; and Da Derga, its master, was delighted and honoured by the visit from the High King.

The pirates having plundered Tara took to their vessels, and having laden them with their spoils were now under a favourable breeze running along the sea coast towards the Hill of Howth, when they perceived from afar the king's company making in their chariots for Dublin along the great high road. One of his own foster-brothers was the first to recognize that it was the High King who was there. He was kept in view and seen at last to enter Da Derga's great court of hospitality. The pirates ran their ships ashore to the south of the Liffey, and Ingcel the Briton set off as a spy to examine the court and the number of armed men about it, to see if it might not be possible to surprise and plunder it during the night. On his return he is questioned by his companions as to what he saw, and by this simple device—familiar to all poets from Homer down—we are introduced to the principal characters of the court, and are shown what the retinue of a High King consisted of, in the sixth or seventh century, about which time the saga probably took definite form, or in the second or third century, if we are to suppose the traits there preserved to be more archaic than the composition of the tale itself. We have here a minute account of the king and the court and the company, with their costumes, insignia

---

* A constant rendezvous for pedestrians and bicyclists from Dublin, not one in ten thousand of whom know the origin of the name or its history.

and appearance. We see the king and his sons, his nine pipers or wind-instrument players, his cup-bearers, his chief druid-juggler, his three principal charioteers, their nine apprentice charioteers, his hostages the Saxon princes, his equerries and out-riders, his three judges, his nine harpers, his three ordinary jugglers, his three cooks, his three poets, his nine guardsmen, and his two private table attendants. We see Da Derga the lord of the court, his three door-keepers, the British outlaws and the king's private drink-bearers.   Here is the description of the king himself:

"I saw there a couch," continued Ingcel, "and its ornamentation was more beautiful than all the other couches of the court; it is curtained round with silver cloth, and the couch itself is richly ornamented.   I saw three persons on it. The outside two of them were fair, both hair and eyebrows, and their skin whiter than snow.   Upon the cheeks of each was a beautiful ruddiness.   Between them in the middle was a noble champion.   He has in his visage the ardour and action of a sovereign, and the wisdom of an historian. The cloak which I saw upon him can be likened only to the mist of a May morning.   A different colour and complexion are seen in it each moment, more splendid than the other is each hue.   I saw in the cloak in front of him a wheel-broach of gold, that reaches from his chin to his waist.   Like unto the shine of burnished gold is the colour of his hair.   Of all the human forms of the world that I have seen his is the most splendid.*   I saw his gold-hilted sword laid down near him.   There

---

* Keating says that according to some, Conairé reigned only thirty years, and from this eulogium on his shapeliness the author of the Saga seems to have followed this tradition.

was the breadth of a man's hand of the sword exposed
out of the scabbard.   From that hand's breadth the
man who sits at the far end of the house could see
even the smallest object by the light of that sword.*
More melodious is the melodious sound of that sword
than the melodious sounds of the golden pipes which
play music in the royal house. . . .   The noble warrior
was asleep with his legs upon the lap of one of the
men, and his head in the lap of the other.   He
awoke afterwards out of his sleep, and spoke these
words :

'I have dreamed of danger-crowding phantoms,
    A host of creeping, treacherous enemies,
    A combat of men beside the Dodder,
    And early and alone the king of Tara was killed.'"

This man whom Ingcel had seen was no other
than the High King.

The account of the juggler is also curious :

" I saw there," continued Ingcel, " a large champion
in the middle of the house.   The blemish of baldness
was upon him.   Whiter than the cotton of the mountains is every hair that grows upon his head.   He had
ear-clasps of gold in his ears and a speckled white
cloak upon him.   He had nine swords in his hands,
and nine silvery shields, and nine balls of gold.   He
throws every one of them up into the air and not one
falls to the ground, and there is but one of them at a
time upon his palm, and like the buzzing of bees on a
beautiful day was the motion of each passing the other."

---

* The allusion is evidently to a bright steel sword in an age
of bronze.   Perhaps the music referred to means the vibration of
the steel when struck.   The "sword of light" is a common
feature in Gaelic folk-lore.

"Yes," said Ferrogain [the foster brother], "I recognise him : he is Tulchinne, the royal druid of the King of Tara. He is Conairé's juggler *—a man of great power is that man."

Da Derga himself is thus described :—"I saw another couch there, and one man on it, with two pages in front of him, one fair, the other black-haired. The champion himself had red hair, and had a red cloak near him. He had crimson cheeks and beautiful deep blue eyes, and had on him a green cloak. He wore also a white under-mantle and collar beautifully interwoven, and a sword with an ivory hilt was in his hand; and he supplies every couch in the court with ale and food, and he is incessant in attending upon the whole company. Identify that man ? "

"I know that man," said he, "that is Da Derga himself. It was by him the court was built, and since he has taken up residence in it its doors have never been closed, except the side to which the wind blows—it is to that side only that a door is put. Since he has taken to housekeeping, his boiler has never been taken off the fire, but continues ever to boil food for the men of Erin. And the two who are in front of him are two boys, foster sons of his; they are the two sons of the King of Leinster."

Not less interesting is the true Celtic hyperbole in Ingcel's description of the jesters :—"I saw there three jesters at the fire. They wore three dark grey cloaks, and if all the men of Erin were in one place, and though the body of the mother or the father of each man of them were lying dead before him, not one of them could refrain from laughing at them."

---

* "Cleasamhnach," from *cleas*, a trick, a common word still.

1

In the end the pirates decided on making their attack. They marched swiftly and silently across the Dublin mountains, surrounded and surprised the court, slew the High King caught there in their trap, and butchered most of his attendants.

After this tale of Da Derga come a host of sagas, all calling for some recognition in a chapter devoted to an account of miscellaneous story. Of these, one of the most important, though neither the longest nor the most interesting, is the account of the Boromean or Boru tribute, a large fragment of which is preserved in the *Book of Leinster*, a MS. of about the year 1150.

When Tuathal or Toole, called *Techtmhar*, or "the Possessor," was High King of Ireland, he had two handsome daughters, and the King of Leinster asked one of them in marriage, and took and brought home to his palace the elder as his wife. This was as it should be, for at that time it was not customary for the younger to be married "before the face of the elder." The Leinstermen, however, said to their king that he had left behind the better girl of the two. Nettled at this the king went again to Tara, and told Tuathal that his daughter was dead, and asked for the other. The High King then gave him his second daughter, with the courteous assurance— "had I one-and-fifty daughters they were thine." When he brought back the second daughter to his palace in Leinster, she, like another Philomela, discovered her sister alive and before her. Both died, one of shame and the other of grief. When news of this reached Tara, steps were taken to punish the King of Leinster. Connacht and Ulster led a great hosting with twelve thousand men into Leinster to plunder it. The High King, too, marched from Tara through Maynooth to Naas, and encamped there. The Leinstermen first beat the Ultonians and killed their king, but all the invading forces having combined, defeated them and slew the bigamist monarch. They then levied the blood-tax, which was as follows :—Fifteen thousand cows, fifteen thousand swine, fifteen thousand wethers, the same number of mantles, silver chains, and copper cauldrons, together with one great copper reservoir to be set in Tara's house itself, in which could fit twelve pigs and twelve kine. In addition to this, they had to pay thirty red-eared cows with calves of the same colour, with halters and spancels of bronze and bosses of gold.

Mál, the successor of Tuathal, again levied this tribute, so did Félim the lawgiver. "Then," says the history, "after many battles Félim's son, Conn, lifted it, Conn's son-in-law Conairé took it, then Art [son of Conn] began to reign, and demanded the Boru tribute, but never secured it without a battle. Art's son, Cormac, lifted it, and so, one year, did Fergus Blacktooth."

The account being evidently a Leinster compilation passes lightly over the occasions on which the tribute was levied, but deals lovingly upon those where the resistance was successful, especially the battle of Cnámhros, or Bone-wood, where Finn and the Fenians helped the Leinstermen against Carbry of the Liffey, and on the battle of Dún-bolg, or Sack-fort, where the celebrated King of Leinster, Brandubh, destroyed the High King of Ireland and his army.

The ruse whereby he got rid of the men of Ulster who had come with the High King, is first described, and afterwards the preparations the men of Leinster made for battle. It was by acting on Bishop Aidan's

advice that Brandubh, the Leinster king, was successful.*

THE BATTLE OF CNAMHROS.

"'Let the very greatest of candles,' said the
bishop, "be dipped in the outer ditch of the rath,
let twelve hundred teams, of twelve oxen each, be
brought to the king; upon these teams let white
creels be laid which shall hold a great number of
warriors who shall be covered with straw, and over all
let there be placed a real layer of provisions. Let a
hundred and fifty unbroken horses be brought thee
moreover, and let bags be fastened to their tails, for
the purpose of stampeding the horse-herds of the King
of Ireland, and let the bags be filled with pebbles.
Let that great taper with the cauldron round its head
shading it, go before thee until thou gain the centre
of the High King's camp. In the meantime send the
High King a message to say that to-night the provisions
of Leinster will be supplied to him.'"

[The further movements of Brandubh, the Leinster
king are then described, and how he slew in single
combat the chief over the stud of the High King. Then
continues the narrative—the Leinster king said :]

"'Can I get,' said he, 'a man to go spy out the
encampment and the king, and who shall be there
waiting for us till we arrive ; and there shall be a
certain fee for that—Heaven from Leinster's clerics,
if he be killed, and if he escape his own land-district

* Standish Hayes O'Grady has published the text of the Boru
tribute in his recent *Silva Gadelica,* accompanied by a masterly
and graphic translation. I give my own translation here, however, though for no better reason than that I had the trouble of
making it.

free to him, and a place at my table to himself and those who come after him.'

" ' I'll go there,' said Rón Cerr, son of Dubánach. son of the King of Imale. 'Give me now,' said he, ' a calf's blood and some rye dough that they be rubbed over me. Give me, too, an ample cowl and wallet.' Thus was it done, so that he was like any leper. A wooden leg was given him, and he placed his knee into its cleft.

" In this guise he departed, and a sword beneath his dress, and came to the place where were the nobles of Erin in the door of the tent of Aedh mac Ainmireach the High King. They asked tidings of him, and 'twas what he said that he was after coming from Kill Bhélat. ' I went since morning,' said he, ' to Leinster's encampment and came back, and my hut and my quern, and my great spade, and my church were destroyed [in my absence].'

" ' Twenty milch cows from me to pay for that,' said the King of Erin, 'if I escape out of this hosting; and do you go over now to yon tent, and the place of nine men to you, and the tenth of my share, and the fragments of the household. What are the Leinster-men doing ?' said the king.

" ' They are preparing food for you, and ye never got food ye shall be more satiated with ! They are boiling their swine and their beeves and their fat hogs.'

" ' Curse on them for it,' cried the men of the race of Owen and Conall.

" ' Two warrior's eyes in the leper's head is what I see,'* said the king.

" ' Woe to you and to your confidence in holding the

---

* The bitter *double entendre* in the last answer of the leper had evidently roused the king's suspicions.

kingship of Erin, if it be at my eyes that fear comes
on you !'

" 'Not so at all,' said the king, 'but let one go now
for Dubhdún, King of Oriel.'

" Thereafter Dubhdún arrived, and the King of Erin
said to him, 'Go,' said the King of Erin, 'and
Oriel's battalion with thee to the foot of Aifé south-
ward, and to the *cruadabhall* and keep watch there
that Leinster make no camp-assault upon us.' They
accordingly proceeded as Aedh the High King ordered
them."

[After a good deal of matter bearing on the High
King's past history, the narrative returns to Brandubh
and the Leinstermen in the following terms :]

" Now about Brandubh ; his horse-herds and ox-
teams are shouted at, and he drew up his battalions
and he marched forward with the darkness of night until
the men of Oriel heard the trot-trot and the roar of
the great host, and the snorting of the horse-herds,
and the puffing of the oxen under the waggons. The
men of Oriel rose up under arms. 'Who is here ?'
said the men of Oriel.

" 'Easy told,' was the answer, 'the gillies of
Leinster with food for the King of Erin.'

" The men of Oriel rose up, and the hand that each
man would put down, he would find either a pig or
a beef under it. 'It's true for them,' said the King
of Oriel, 'let them pass by.' 'Let us go too,' said
the men of Oriel, 'let not our share of the victuals be
forgotten.' The men of Oriel accordingly proceeded
to their encampment huts.

" The men of Leinster went on to 'the hill of the
candle' in the very middle of the King of Erin's
camp, and there they take the cauldron from about the
candle.

"'What light is that I see?' said the king.

"'Easy told,' said the leper, 'it's the arrival of the provisions.'

"The leper arose, knocked off his wooden leg, and reached his hand to his sword. Their loads were taken off the ox-teams and the horses were let loose amongst the steeds of the men of Erin, so that they went into a stampede and broke down both huts and tents of the men of Erin. The Leinstermen rose up out of their baskets like a deluging river over cliffs, in their grasp their sword-hilts, by their straps their shields, on their sides their mail.

"'Who is here?' cried the men of Clan Conall and Clan Owen.

"'The dealers out of the food,' said the leper.

"'God bless us,' said each man, 'why they are a multitude!'

"Up rose the men of Clan Conall and Clan Owen, and though they did, they were like hands thrust into a nest of serpents. A pen of spears and shields were made by them round the King of Erin, and he was forced on his steed and carried by them to the 'Gap of Shields.' The shields of the men of Erin, were cast away by them and abandoned at the mouth of that gap [and hence its name]. Rón Cerr [the pretended leper] makes a rush at the King of Erin, and kills nine men in his efforts to get at him. Then Dubhdún, King of Oriel, came between them, and he and Rón Cerr fight, and Dubhdún falls by him. Rón Cerr again makes an assault on the King of Erin, and Fergus, son of Flaithri, King of Tulach Óg, comes between them, and Fergus falls by Rón Cerr. After that Rón Cerr again makes a rush for the king and seizes him by the leg and drags him down towards him from off his horse, and takes his head off him on the 'flag

of bone-bruising.'   Then he seizes his wallet and
pours the food-scraps out of it and puts the head into
it, and gets him away secretly to the mountain plains
and remains there till morning.

"Howsoever, Leinster follows after Conn's half [*i.e.*,
the Northerns], and makes a red-killing of them.
On the morrow each arrived after slaughter and
triumphs to the spot where Brandubh was, and Rón
Cerr, too, comes and lays down before him the head of
Aedh mac Ainmireach, the High King of Ireland.   So
that is the battle of Bolgdún fought for the Boru
tribute.   In that battle Bec mac Cuanach was slain."

The following sagas and romances are amongst those
which may be classed as miscellaneous :—The Courtship of Etain ; The Courtship of Crunn's Wife ;   The
Battle of Moy Rath ;* The Voyage of Maelduin ;† The
Voyage of the Sons of O'Corra ; ‡ The Tragical Death
of Maelfathartaigh (Mael-faharty) son of Ronan (king
of Leinster, A.D. 610) ; The Elopement of Erc, daughter of Loarn ; The Slaughter of Cairbré Cat head by
the Free Clans of Erin ; The Battle of Ath Cumair ;
The Triumphs of Congal Clairingneach ; The Love
of Dubhlucha for Mongan ; The Expedition of Daithi
(last Pagan King of Ireland) to the Alps ; The Progress
of the Deisi from Tara ; The Dream of Mac Cong-
linné ;§ The Plunder of the City of Mael Mil-sgo-
thach, a sort of allegory, and others.

---

* Published in 1842 by O'Donovan for the Archæological Society.

† Translated, but not quite literally, by Dr. Joyce in his *Early
Celtic Romances*, from which Tennyson took the subject of his
well-known poem, "The Voyage of Maeldune."

‡ Translated in Dr. Joyce's last Edition.

§ A curious tenth or twelfth century burlesque recently
edited by Kuno Meyer.

CHAPTER XI.

THE OSSIANIC POEMS.

IDE by side with the numerous prose stories which fall under the head of "Fenian," exists an enormous mass of poems, chiefly narrative, of a minor epic type, intermingled with others whose basis is a semi-dramatic dialogue between St. Patrick and Ossian. This poet was fabled to have lived in Tír-na-n-óg* or the "land of the ever-young," for three hundred years, thus surviving all the Fenians, and living to hold colloquy with St. Patrick. The Ossianic poems are extraordinarily numerous, and if they were all collected would probably amount to some fifty thousand lines—the much-lamented Father Keegan estimated them once, but I think hardly correctly, at one hundred thousand. They are written in rather irregular metres, for the most part imitations of Deibhidh and

* Pronounced *"t'neer na nogue,"* *"nogue"* rhyming to *"rogue."*

Rannaigheacht Mhór,* chiefly the latter, and were, even down to our own time, exceedingly popular in both Ireland and the Scotch Highlands, in which last country Campbell of Islay made the great collection, chiefly from oral sources, which he called Leabhar na Féinne or the Book of the Fenians.

Some of the Ossianic poems relate the exploits of the Fenians; others describe conflicts between some of that body and dragons; others tell of fights with monsters and with strangers come from across the sea; others detail how Finn and his companions suffered from the enchantments of wizards, and the efforts made to release them; one enumerates the Fenians who fell at Cnoc-an-áir; another gives the names of some three hundred of the Fenian hounds; another gives Ossian's account of his three hundred years in the Land of the Young and his return; many more consist largely of semi-humourous dialogues between the Saint and the old warrior; another is called Ossian's madness; another is Ossian's account of the' Battle of Gowra which made an end of the Fenians, and so on.†

The Lochlannachs or Norsemen figure very largely in these poems, and it is quite evident that most of them—at least in the modern form in which we now have them—are post-Norse productions. The fact that the language in which they have for the most part

* For an explanation of these metres, pronounced D'yevvee and "Ran-ee-ught Wore," see my forthcoming *Báird agus Bárduigheacht*.

† Standish Hayes O'Grady in his preface to the third volume of the Ossianic Society's publications gives the names of thirty-five of these poems, amounting to between ten and eleven thousand lines, but many are omitted from this list. In the fragmentary *Dialogue of the Sages* alone there are very nearly two thousand lines of verse mingled with the prose story.

come down to us is popular and modern, does not prove much one way or the other, for these small epics which, more than any other part of Irish literature, were handed down from father to son and propagated orally, have had their language unconsciously adjusted from age to age so as to leave them intelligible to their hearers. As a consequence the metres have in many places also suffered, and the old Irish system, which required a certain number of syllables in each line, has shown signs of fusing gradually with the new Irish system which only requires so many accented syllables.

It is, however, perfectly possible—as has been supposed by, I think, Mr. Nutt and others—that after the terrible shock given to the island by the Northmen, this people usurped in our ballads the place of some older mythical race, and Prof. Rhys was I believe at one time of opinion that Lochlann, as spoken of in these ballads, originally meant merely the country of lochs and seas, and that the Lochlanners were a submarine mythical people like the Fomorians.

The spirit of banter with which St. Patrick and the Church is treated and in which the fun just stops short of irreverence, is a mediæval, not a primitive trait; more characteristic, thinks Mr. Nutt, of the twelfth than of any succeeding century. We all remember the inimitable felicity with which that great English-speaking Gael, Sir Walter Scott,* has caught this Ossianic tone in the lines which Hector McIntyre repeats for the Antiquary :—

Patrick the psalm-singer,
Since you will not listen to one of my stories,

* Both the Buccleugh Scotts and the other four branches of the name were originally Gaelic-speaking Celts.

Though you never heard it before,
I am sorry to tell you,
You are little better than an ass.

To which the Saint, to the infinite contempt of the unbelieving Oldbuck, is made to respond :—

Upon my word, son of Fingal,
While I am warbling the psalms,
The clamour of your old woman's tales,
Disturbs my devotional exercises.

Whereat the heated Ossian retorts :—

Dare you compare your psalms
To the tales of the bare-armed Fenians,
I shall think it no great harm
To wring your bald head from your shoulders.

Here, however, is a real specimen from the Irish which will give some idea of the style of dialogue between the pair. St. Patrick with exaggerated episcopal severity, having Ossian three quarters starved, quite blind, and wholly at his mercy, desires him not to speak of Finn or the Fenians.

OSSIAN.

Alas ! O Patrick, I did think that God would not be angered thereat. I think long, and it is a great woe to me, not to speak of the way of Finn of the Deeds.

PATRICK.

Speak not of Finn nor of the Fenians, for the Son of God will be angry with thee for it, He would never let thee into His fort, and He would not send thee the bread of each day.

OSSIAN.

Were I to speak of Finn and of the Fenians, between us two, O Patrick the new, but only not to speak loud, he would never hear us mentioning them.

PATRICK.

Let nothing whatever be mentioned by thee excepting the offering of God, or if thou talkest continually of others, thou indeed shalt not go to the house of the saints.

OSSIAN.

I will O Patrick do his will. Of Finn or of the Fenians I shall not talk, for fear of bringing anger upon them, O Cleric, since it be God's wont to be angry.

In another poem St. Patrick denounces with still greater vigour.

PATRICK.

Finn is in hell in bonds, "the pleasant man who used to bestow gold," in penalty of his disobedience to God, he is now in the house of pain in sorrow. . . .

Because of the amusement he had with the hounds, and for attending the (bardic) schools each day, and because he took no heed of God, Finn of the Fenians is in bonds. . . .

Misery attend thee, old man, who speakest words of madness, God is better for one hour than all the Fenians of Erin.

OSSIAN.

O Patrick of the crooked crozier, who makest me that impertinent answer, thy crozier would be in atoms were Oscar present.

Were my son Oscar and God hand to hand on

Knock na-veen, if I saw my son down, it is then I would say that God was a strong man.

How could it be that God and His clerics could be better men than Finn, the chief King of the Fenians, the generous one who was without blemish?

All the qualities that you and your clerics say are according to the rule of the king of the stars, Finn's Fenians had them all, and they must be now stoutly seated in God's heaven.

Were there a place, above or below, better than heaven, 'tis there Finn would go, and all the Fenians he had. . . .

Patrick, enquire of God whether He recollects when the Fenians were alive, or hath He seen, east or west, men their equal in the time of fight?

Or hath He seen in His own country, though high it be above our heads, in conflict, in battle, or in might, a man who was equal to Finn?

PATRICK.

[exhausted with controversy, and curious for Ossian's story.]

> Ossian, sweet to me thy voice,
>> Now blessings choice on the soul of Finn!
> But tell to us how many deer
>> Were slain at Slieve-na-man finn.*

OSSIAN.

We, the Fenians, never used to tell untruth; a lie was never attributed to us. By truth and the strength of our hands we used to come safe out of every danger.

---

* This is the usual metre of these poems, but I have translated the mellifluous verses of the dialogue into prose, which always conveys the sense better.

There never sat cleric in church, though melodiously ye may think they chant psalms, more true to his word than the Fenians, the men who shrank never from fierce conflicts.

. . . . . .

O Patrick, where was thy God the day the two came across the sea, who carried off the Queen of the King of Lochlann in ships, by whom many fell here in conflict?

Or when Tailc mac Treoin arrived, the man who put great slaughter on the Fenians? 'Twas not by God the hero fell, but by Oscar in the presence of all.

Many a battle, victory, and contest were celebrated by the Fenians of Innisfail. I never heard that any feat was performed by the King of Saints, or that He reddened His hand.

PATRICK.

Let us cease disputing on both sides, thou withered old man who art devoid of sense; understand that God dwells in heaven of the orders, and Finn and his hosts are all in pain.

OSSIAN.

Great, then, would be the shame for God not to release Finn from the shackles of pain, for if God Himself were in bonds my chief would fight for him.

Finn never suffered in his day any one to be in pain or difficulty without redeeming him by silver or gold, or by battle and fight, until he was victorious.

It is a good claim I have against your God, me to be amongst His clerics as I am, without food, without clothing or music, without bestowing gold on bards.

Without bathing, without hunting, without Finn, without courting generous women, without sport, without sitting in my place as was due, without learning feats of agility and conflict, etc.

Many of these poems contain lyrical passages of great beauty. Here, as a specimen, is Ossian's description of the things in which Finn used to take delight. It is a truly lyrical passage, in the very best style, rhyme, rhythm, and assonance all combined with a most rich vocabulary of words expressive of sounds nearly impossible to translate into English. It might be thus attempted in verse, though not quite in the metre of the original. Finn's pursuits, as depicted here by Ossian, show him to have been, like all true Gaels, a lover of Nature, and are quite in keeping with his own poem on Spring; his are indeed the tastes of one of Matthew Arnold's "Barbarians" glorified.

FINN'S PASTIMES.

Oh, croaking Patrick, I curse your tale,
　Is the king of the Fenians in hell this night?
The heart that never was seen to quail,
　That feared no danger and felt no spite.

What kind of a God can be yours, to grudge
　Bestowing of food on him, giving of gold?
Finn never refused either prince or drudge,—
　Can his doom be in hell, in the house of cold? *

* In the original—

　　　αn éαʒcóιη nαċ mαιċ ʟe Ɗια
　　　Óη α'η bιαɒh ɒo ċhαbhαιηc ɒo neαch?
　　　Níoη ɒhιúʟcαιʒh Fιonn cηeun nά cηuαʒh
　　　Iηηιonn ηuαη mά 'η é α ċheαch.

Irish writers always describe hell as cold, not hot. This is so even in Keating, the "cold flag of hell."

The desire of my hero, who feared no foe,
    Was to listen all day to Drumderrig's sound,
To sleep by the roar of the Assaroe,
    And to follow the dun deer round and round.

The warbling of blackbirds in Letter Lee,
    The strand where the billows of Ruree fall,
The bellowing ox upon wild Moy-mee,
    The lowing of calves upon Glen-da-Vaul.

The blast ot a horn around Slieve Grot,
    The bleat of a fawn upon Cua's plain,
The sea-bird's cry in a lonely spot,
    The croak of the raven above the slain.

The thud of the waves on his bark afar,
    The yelp of the pack as they round Drumliss,
The baying of Bran upon Knock-in-ar,
    The murmur of fountains below Slieve Mis.

The call of Oscar upon the chase,*
    The tongue of the hounds on the Fenians' plain,
Then a seat with the men of the bardic race—
    Of these delights was my hero fain.

* In the original—

     Glaoḋ Orcaır ag ꝺul ꝺo ṗeilg,
      Goċa gaꝺar ar leirg na ḃꝼıann,
    Ḃeıċ 'nna ṗuıꝺhe amearg na nꝺáṁh
      Ḃa h-é rın ꝺe ghnáċh a mhıan

    Mıan ꝺe mhıanaıḃ Orcaır ṗéıl
      Ḃeıċ ag éırceaċc ꝛe béım rgıaċh,
    Ḃeıċ ı gcaċ ag corgar cnáṁh
      Ḃa h-é rın ꝺe ghnáċh a mhıan.

But generous Oscar's supreme desire
   Was the maddening clashing of shield to shield,
And the hewing of bones in the battle ire,
   And the crash and the joy of the stricken field.

In entire accordance with this enthusiastic love of
Nature is Ossian's delightful ode to the Blackbird of
Derrycarn, a piece which is generally found in the
MSS. standing by itself. Interpenetrated with the
same sensations of delight at the sights and sounds of
Nature are the following verses attributed to him,
which a Scotchman, Dean Macgregor, jotted down
in phonetic spelling, just as he heard them some 380
years ago, doubtless from the recitation of some wan-
dering bard or harper :—

OSSIAN SANG.

Sweet is the voice in the land of gold,*
   And sweeter the music of birds that soar,
When the cry of the heron is heard on the wold,
   And the waves break softly on Bundatrore.

Down floats on the murmuring of the breeze
   The call of the cuckoo from Cossahun,
The blackbird is warbling among the trees,
   And soft is the kiss of the warming sun.

---

* See p. 59 of the Gaelic part of *Book of the Dean of Lismore*.
The first verse runs thus in modern Irish :—

      binn guch duine i dtír an óir
       binn an glór chanaid na h-eóin
      binn an nuallan a gnídh an chorr
      binn an tonn i mbun-da-treóir.

The cry of the eagle of Assaroe
O'er the court of Mac Morne to me is sweet,
And sweet is the cry of the bird below
Where the wave and the wind and the tall cliff meet.

Finn mac Cool is the father of me,
Whom seven battalions of Fenians fear.
When he launches his hounds on the open lea,
Grand is their cry as they rouse the deer.

Caoilte (Cweelt-ya) too, like his friends Finn and Ossian, seems to have been very impressionable to the various moods of Nature. Here is the literal translation made by Standish Hayes O'Grady of his lyrical description of Winter in the Dialogue of the Sages, or "Colloquy of the Ancients," as O'Grady prefers to translate it. "Upon the whole province," says the prose introduction, "distress of cold settled, and heavy snow came down, so that it reached men's shoulders and the axle-trees of chariots, and of the russet forest branches made a twisting-together, as it had been of withes, so that men might not progress there," then Caoilte made this lay.

A Winter Night.

Cold the winter night is, the wind is risen, the high-couraged unquelled stag is on foot: bitter cold to-night the whole mountain is, yet for all that the ungovernable stag is belling.*

---

* This, like most of the 2,000 lines of poetry scattered through the Colloquy, is in the Deibhidh (D'yevvee) metre, and might be thus translated into that metre in English :—

Cold the **W**inter, cold the **W**ind,
The **R**aging stag is **R**ávin'd,
Though in one **Flag** the **F**loodgates cling
The **S**teaming **Stag** is bélling.

The deer of Slievecarn of the gatherings commits not his side to the ground, no less than he, the stag of frigid Echtgé's summit (who) catches the chorus of the wolves.

I, Caoilte, with Brown Diarmuid and with keen light-footed Oscar; we too in the nipping night's waning end would listen to the music of the [wolf] pack.

But well the red deer sleeps that with his hide to the bulging rock lies stretched—hidden as though beneath the country's surface—all in the latter end of chilly night, etc.

There is a considerable thread of narrative running through these poems, and connecting them in a kind of series, so that several of them might be divided into the various books of a Gaelic epic of the Odyssic type, containing, instead of the wanderings and final restoration of Ulysses, the adventures and final destruction of the Fenians, except that the books would be rather more disjointed. There is, moreover, splendid material for an ample epic in the division between the Fenians of Munster and Connacht, and the gradual estrangement of the High King, leading up to the fatal Battle of Gowra, but the material for this last exists chiefly in prose texts, not in the Ossianic lays. It is very strange and very unfortunate that, notwithstanding the literary activity of Gaelic Ireland before and during the Penal times, no Keating or Comyn or Curtin ever attempted to redact the Ossianic poems and throw them into that epic form into which they would so easily and naturally have fitted. These pieces appear to me of great value as showing the natural growth and genesis of an epic, for we progressed just up to the point of possessing a large mass of stray material and minor episodes versified by anonymous long-forgotten folk-poets, but never produced a mind critical enough to reduce this mass to order, coherence, and stability, and at the same time creative enough to supply the necessary lacunæ. Were it not that so much light has by this time been thrown upon the natural genesis of ancient national epics, one might be inclined to lay down the theory that the Irish had evolved a scheme of their own, peculiar to themselves, and different altogether from the epic, a scheme in which the same characters figure in a group of allied poems and romances, each of which is perfect in itself, and not dependent upon the rest, a system afterwards developed in Tennyson's *Idylls*, and one which might be taken to be a natural result of the impatient Celtic spirit which could not brook the restraints of the epic.

The Ossianic lays are almost the only narrative poems which exist in the language, for although lyrical elegiac, and didactic poetry abounds, the Irish never produced, except in the case of the Ossianic epopees, anything of importance in a narrative and ballad form, anything, for instance, of the nature of the glorious ballad poetry of the Scotch Lowlands.

The Ossianic metres, too, are the eminently epic ones of Ireland. It was a great pity, and, to my thinking, a great mistake, for Archbishop MacHale not to have used them in his translation of Homer, instead of attempting it in the metre of Pope's *Iliad*— one utterly unknown to native Ireland.

I have already observed that great producers of literature as the Irish always were, until this century, they never developed a drama. The nearest approach to such a thing is in these Ossianic poems. The dialogue between St. Patrick and Ossian, of which in most of the Ossianic poems, there is either more or

less, is quite dramatic in its form.   Even the reciters
of the present day feel this, and I have heard the cen-
sorious, self-satisfied tone of Patrick, and the vin-
dictive whine of the half-starved old man, reproduced
with considerable humour by a reciter.   But I think
it nearly certain—though just now I cannot prove it
—that in former days there was real acting and a
dialogue between two persons, one representing the
Saint and the other the old Pagan.   It was from a less
promising beginning than this that the drama of
Æschylus developed.   But nothing could develop in
Ireland.   Everything, time after time, was arrested in
its growth.   Again and again the tree of Irish literature
put forth fresh blossoms, and before they could fully
expand they were nipped off.   The conception of
bringing the spirit of Paganism and of Christianity
together in the persons of the last great poet and
warrior of the one, and the first great saint of the
other, was truly dramatic, and the spirit and humour with which it has been carried out in the
pieces which have come down to us, are a strong
presumption that under happier circumstances something very great would have developed from it.   If
anyone is still found to repeat Macaulay's hackneyed
taunt about our race never having produced a great
poem, let him ask himself if it is likely that a country
where, for a hundred years after Aughrim and the
Boyne, teachers, who for long before that had been in
great danger, were systematically knocked on the head
or sent to a jail for teaching ; where children were seen
learning their letters with chalk on their fathers' tombstones, other means being denied them ; where the
possession of a manuscript might lead to the owner's
death or imprisonment, so that many valuable books
were buried in the ground or hidden to rot in walls—

whether such a country were a soil on which an epic or anything else could flourish. How, in the face of all this, the men of the eighteenth century preserved in manuscript so much of the Ossianic poetry as they did, and even re-wrote or redacted portions of it, as Michael Comyn is said to have done to " Ossian in the Land of the Young," is to me nothing short of amazing.

Of the authorship of the Ossianic poems nothing is known. In the *Book of Leinster* are three short pieces ascribed to Ossian himself, and five to Finn, and other old MSS. contain poems ascribed to Caoilte (Cweelt-ya), Ossian's companion and fellow-survivor, but of the great mass of the ten or twenty thousand lines which we have in seventeenth and eighteenth century MSS. there is not much which is placed in Ossian's mouth at first hand, the pieces, as I have said, gener- ally beginning with a dialogue, from which Ossian proceeds to recount his tale. But this dramatic form of the lay shows that no pretence was kept up of Ossian's being the singer of his own exploits.* From the paucity of the pieces attributed to him in the oldest MSS., it is probable that the Gaelic race only gradually singled him out as their typical Pagan poet instead of Fergus or Caoilte or any other of his alleged contemporaries, just as they singled out his father, Finn, as the typical Pagan leader of their race ; and it is likely that a large part of our Ossianic lay and literature is post-Danish, while the great mass of of the Red Branch saga is in its birth many centuries anterior to the Norsemen's invasion.

* One of the great German scholars, I think Windisch, has suggested that Ossian was first taken to be a poet from having verses put into his mouth in the prose saga. However, the same is quite as true of Caoilte and Fergus.

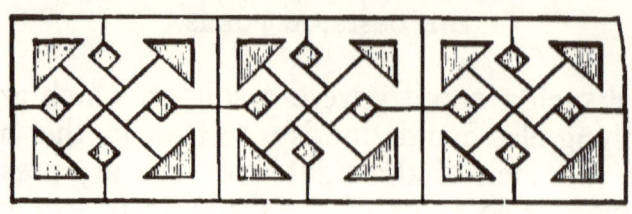

CHAPTER XII.

THE IRISH ANNALS.

O sketch of Irish literature should omit some mention of the Annals, dry and un-literary as most of them are. The Irish Annals, however, are too important, from their value, age and number, to be over-looked. The greatest—though almost the youngest—of them all, is the much-renowned *Annals of the Four Masters*. This mighty work is chiefly due to the herculean labours of the learned Franciscan, Brother Michael O'Clery, a native of Donegal, born about the year 1580, who was himself descended from a long line of scholars.* He and another scion of Donegal, Aedh Mac an Bháird, then guardians of St. Anthony's in Louvain, contemplated the compi-

---

* For an account of how these O'Clerys came to Donegal see the interesting preface to Father Murphy's splendid edition of the Irish-Gaelic *Life of Red Hugh O'Donnell.*

lation and publication of a great collection of the lives of the Irish saints.

In furtherance of this idea, Michael O'Clery, with the leave and approbation of his superiors, set out from Louvain, and, coming to Ireland, travelled through the whole length and breadth of it, from abbey to abbey and friary to friary. Up and down, high and low, he hunted for the ancient vellum books and time-stained manuscripts, whose safety was even then threatened by the ever-thickening political shocks and spasms of that most distracted age. These, whenever he found, he copied in an accurate and beautiful handwriting, and transmitted safely to Louvain to his friend Mac an Bháird, or " Ward," as the name is now in English. Ward, unfortunately, died before he could make use of the material thus collected by O'Clery, but it was taken up by another great Franciscan, Father John Colgan, who utilised the work of his friend O'Clery by producing in 1645 two huge and splendid Latin quartos, the first called the *Trias Thaumaturgus*, containing the lives of Saints Patrick, Brigit, and Columkille, the second containing all the lives which could be found of all the Irish saints whose festivals fell between the 1st of January and the last of March.

Before O'Clery ever entered the Franciscan Order he had been by profession an historian or antiquary, and now, in his eager quest for ecclesiastical writings and the lives of saints, his trained eye fell upon many other documents which he could not neglect. These were the ancient books and secular annals of the nation, and the historical poems of the ancient bards. He indulged himself to the full in this unique opportunity to become acquainted with so much valuable material, and the results of his labours are two valuable

books, the *Réim Rioghraidhe*,* or Succession of King
in Ireland, which gives the name, succession, and
genealogy of the Kings of Ireland from the earliest
times down to the death of Malachy the Great in
1022, giving at the same time the genealogies of the
early saints of Ireland down to the eighth century; and
the *Leabhar Gabhála*,* or Book of Invasions, which
contains an ample account of the successive coloniza-
tions of Ireland which were made by Partholan, the
Nemedians, the Tuatha de Dananns, etc., all drawn
from ancient books—for the most part now lost—and
digested and put together by the friar.

It was probably while engaged on this work that the
great scheme of compiling the Annals of Ireland
occurred to him. He found a patron and protector
in Fergal O'Gara, lord of Moy-Gara and Coolavin, and
with the assistance of five or six other antiquaries he
set about his task, in the secluded Convent of
Donegal, at that time governed by his own brother.
He began his work on the 22nd of January, 1632,
and finished it on the 10th of August, 1636; having
had, during all this time, his expenses and the expenses of his fellow-labourers defrayed by the patriotic
lord of Moy-Gara.

It was Father Colgan who first gave this great work
the title under which it is now always spoken of—
The Annals of the Four Masters. Father Colgan,
in the preface to his *Acta Sanctorum Hiberniæ*, after
recounting O'Clery's labours and his previous books,
goes on to give an account of this last one also, and
adds: "As in the three works before mentioned, so
in this fourth one, three [helpers of his] are eminently
to be praised—namely, Farfassa O'Mulconry, Pere-

---

* Pronounced "*Raim Ree-ree-a*" and "*L'yowar Gow-aul-a.*"

grine * O'Clery, and Peregrine O'Duigenan, men of consummate learning in the antiquities of the country, and of approved faith. And to these were subsequently added the co-operation of other distinguished antiquarians, as Maurice O'Mulconry, who for one month, and Conary O'Clery, who for many months laboured in its promotion. But since those Annals, which we shall very frequently have occasion to quote in this volume and in others following, have been collected and compiled by the assistance and separate study of so many authors, neither the desire of brevity would permit us always to quote them individually, nor would justice permit us to attribute the labour of many to one, hence it sometimes seemed best to call them the Annals of Donegal, for in our convent of Donegal they were commenced and concluded. But afterwards, for other reasons, chiefly for the sake of the compilers themselves, who were four most eminent masters in antiquarian lore, we have been led to call them the ANNALS OF THE FOUR MASTERS. Yet we said just now that more than four assisted in their preparation ; however, as their meeting was irregular, and but two of them during a short time laboured in the unimportant and later part of the work, while the other four were engaged on the entire production at least up to the year 1267 (from which the first part, and the most necessary one for us, is closed), we quote it under their name."

" I explained to you," says Michael O'Clery in his

---

* The Irish Cucoigcriche, which, meaning a "stranger," has been Latinised Peregrinus by Ward. I remember one of the l'Estrange family telling me how one of the O'Cucoigrys had once come to her father and asked him if he had any objection to his translating his name for the future into l'Estrange, both names being identical in meaning !

dedication to Fergal O'Gara, after setting forth the scope
of the work, "that I thought I could get the assistance
of the chroniclers for whom I had most esteem in
writing a book of annals, in which these matters might
be put on record, and that, should the writing of them
be neglected at present, they would not again be found
to be put on record or commemorated even to the
end of the world. All the best and most copious
books of annals that I could find throughout all Ireland
were collected by me—though it was difficult for me
to collect them into one place—to write this book in
your name and to your honour, for it was you who
gave the reward of their labour to the chroniclers, by
whom it was written, and it was the friars of Donegal
who supplied them with food and attendance."

The book is also provided with a kind of testimo-
nium from the Franciscan Fathers of the monastery
where it was written, stating who the compilers were,
and how long they had worked under their own eyes,
and what old books they had seen with them, etc. In
addition to this, Michael O'Clery carried it to the two
historians of greatest eminence in the South of Ireland,
Flann mac Egan, of Ballymacegan, in the County
Tipperary, and Conor mac Brody, of the County
Clare, and obtained their written approbation and
signatures, as well as those of the Primate of Ireland
and some others ; and thus provided he launched his
book upon the world.

It has been published, at least in part, three times—
first, down to the year 1171, the year of the Norman
Invasion, by the Rev. Charles O'Conor, grandson of
Charles O'Conor of Belanagare, Carolan's patron,
with a Latin translation ; and, secondly, in English by
Owen Connellan from the year 1171 to the end. Bu
the third publication of it—that by O'Donovan—was

the greatest work that any modern Irish scholar ever accomplished. In it the Irish text, with accurate English translation, and an enormous quantity of notes, topographical, genealogical, and historical, are given, and the whole is contained in seven huge quarto volumes—a work of which any age or country might be proud. So long as Irish history exists, the *Annals of the Four Masters* will be read in O'Donovan's translation, and the name of O'Donovan be inseparably connected with those of the O'Clerys.

We have left ourselves but little space to notice the contents of these Annals. Suffice it to say that, like so many other compilations of the same kind, they begin with *the Deluge ;* and they end up in the year 1616. They give from the old books the reigns, deaths, genealogies, etc., not only of the High Kings but also of the provincial kings, chiefs, or heads of distinguished families, men of science, and poets, with their respective dates, going as near as they can go. They record deaths and successions of saints, abbots, bishops, and ecclesiastical dignitaries. They tell of the foundation and occasionally of the overthrow of countless churches, castles, abbeys, convents, and religious institutions. They give meagre details of battles and political changes, and occasionally quote ancient verses in proof of facts. Towards the end the dry summary of events becomes more garnished, and in parts elaborate detail takes the place of meagre facts. There is no event of Irish history, from the birth of Christ to the beginning of the seventeenth century, that the first enquiry of the student will not be, "What do the Four Masters say about it?" for the great value of the work consists in this, that we have here, in condensed form, the pith and substance of the old books of Ireland which were then in existence

but which—as the Four Masters foresaw they would—
have long since perished.   The facts and dates of the
Four Masters are not their own facts and dates.   From
confused masses of very ancient matter they, with
labour and much sifting, drew forth their dates and
synchronisms, and harmonized their facts.

As if to emphasize the truth that they were only
redacting the Annals of Ireland from the most
ancient sources at their command, the Masters
wrote in an ancient bardic dialect full of such
idioms and words as were unintelligible even to the
men of their own day unless they had received a
bardic training.   In fact they were learned men
writing for the learned, and this work was one of the
last efforts of the *esprit de corps* of the school-bred
shannachie which always prompted him to keep bardic
and historical learning a close monopoly amongst his
own class.   Keating was Michael O'Clery's contemporary, but he wrote—and I consider him the first
Irish historian and trained scholar who did so—for
the masses not the classes, and he had his reward in
the thousands of copies of his popular history made
and read throughout all Ireland, while the copies
made of the Annals were quite few in comparison and
after the end of the 17th century little read.

The old and valuable *Annals of Tighearnach*, who
died about the year 1088 ; the *Annals of Innisfallen*,
composed about A.D. 1215, but according to O'Curry
commenced at least two centuries before that period ;
the *Annals of Boyle*, beginning with the creation and
continued down to A.D. 1253 ; the *Annals of Ulster*,
covering the period from A.D. 431 to 1504 ; the *Annals
of Loch Ce*, continued from 1014 down to 1590 ; the
fragmentary *Annals of Boyle*, from the year 1224 to

1562 ; the *Annals of Clonmacnois*,* continued down to the year 1408 ; the fragmentary Annals published by O'Donovan, and the celebrated *Chronicon Scotorum* of Duald Mac Firbis, are the other principal Annals of Ireland still existing.

Such books as *The Wars of the Gall with the Gael*, which gives an account of the Danish Invasion and the story of the battle of Clontarf, apparently told by an eye-witness ; the *History of the Wars of Thomond*, compiled about 1459, which tells all about the O'Brien family, their Norman wars and

---

* Now known only through an English translation of it—soon, I hope, to be published—made in 1627 by one Connla mac Echagan of Westmeath for his friend and kinsman Torlogh mac Cochlan, lord of Delvin. The dedication is curious, it runs in a very German kind of fashion :—

" To the worthy and of great expectation young gentleman Mr. Terence Coghlan, his brother Connell Ma Geoghegan wisheth long health with good success in all his affairs."

He says in his preface that formerly many septs lived in Ireland whose profession it was to chronicle and keep in memory the state of the kingdom, but " now as they cannot enjoy that re-pect and gain by their profession as heretofore they and their ancestors received, they set nought by the said knowledge, neglect their books, and choose rather to put their children to learn English than their own native language, insomuch that some of them suffer tailors to cut the leaves of the said books (which their ancestors held in great account) and sew them in long pieces to make their measures of, [so] that the posterities are like to fall into more ignorance of any things which happened before their time."

I should have thought Mac Echagan exaggerated a little here. Certainly it was only after the Cromwellian wars that this state of things became in the least general. It is very remarkable, however, to see a Mac Echagan writing all this to a Mac Coghlan in English, at a time when not one Gael in twenty knew a word of that language. To write finely *in English* about the decay of the Irish language is something we have long been accustomed to ; this is certainly the first instance of it.

their Gaelic and Norman neighbours, and the *Book of Munster*, which is a history of the Southern Irish down to the time of the Battle of Clontarf; all these are more properly books of history than Annals; but as we have no space to assign them a chapter to themselves, and as many of them do not come under the heading of *early* Irish literature, I content myself with mentioning them here; and merely remark that not only are they valuable for their facts, but are all of them books of more interest—from a literary point of view—than the Annals. As the Annals themselves, although many of them are late compilations, are really only digests of very ancient books now lost, I have thought it as well to assign them a chapter in this place.

CHAPTER XIII.

THE EARLY CHRISTIAN WRITERS.

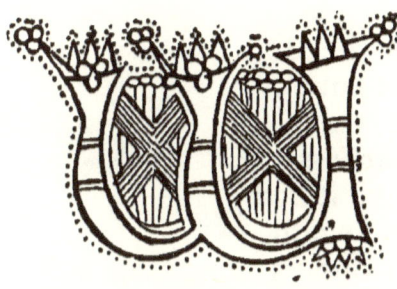ITH Christianity there came into Ireland—as into every other country—a new life, new ideals, a new literature and a new style, which subsisted for many a long day, side by side with Pagan ideals and Pagan literature.

There are several Irish poems attributed to St. Patrick himself, but with the exception of his celebrated Faedh Fiada or Cry of the Deer, which may very well be partly genuine, they are most of them evidently post-Patrician, some—the alleged prophecies —being grotesquely so. The Faedh Fiada consists of eighty lines, short, like those of a litany, and full of fervour. The legend is that when the saint was first summoned to King Laoghaire's [Leary's] presence at Tara, after having insulted him by kindling the Paschal fire within sight of the palace, he was dismissed for that time with scant courtesy, but was afterwards sent for by the king to explain his " new way " to the nobles assembled at Tara. In reality, however, the king laid an ambuscade along the road by which he

L

must come to the palace, intending to have him quietly
knocked on the head during the route, and everything
thus peacefully settled. Patrick, however, who was
accompanied by St. Benignus and eight companions,
assumed, with his followers, in the eyes of the intending murderers the form of deer, and thus came safe to
Tara ; and the hymn which he chanted as he went
along, has been ever since called the Faedh * Fiada or
Cry of the Deer. Most people are familiar with this
poem through Mangan's excellent but very diffuse
verse translation :—

At Tara to-day in this fateful hour
I place all Heaven with its power,
And the sun with its brightness,
And the snow with its whiteness,
And fire with all the strength it hath,
And lightning with its rapid wrath,
And the winds with their swiftness along their path,
And the sea with its deepness,
And the rocks with their steepness,
And the earth with its starkness,
    All these I place
    By God's almighty help and grace,
Between myself and the power of darkness.

This celebrated hymn preserved to us in the 11th
century manuscript called the *Book of Hymns*, is the
first Christian strain heard in Ireland, which has come
floating to us down the ages, and for centuries it was
believed that the recitation of it was a strong defence
against danger of body and soul. To this day in
Aran and elsewhere is heard another similar hymn
the " Marthainn Phádraig," or life-giving prayer of

* The word Faedh is long obsolete.

Patrick, to which the same protective virtue is ascribed.

The most remarkable piece of Irish literature with which the name of St. Patrick is connected is of course the redaction of that division of the Brehon Law called the Cáin Phádraig, consisting of the Senchus Mór or Great Tradition. This was an attempt on Patrick's part to rewrite the body of Pagan Law, or rather to expunge from it what was ultra-Pagan and glaringly anti-Christian. The only way in which he could accomplish his purpose was by consenting to a joint committee of revisal, consisting of three bishops, three kings, and three brehons. Ros the chief Filè and Brehon of Ireland, first arranged the code of previously existing laws, leaving them ready for revision, and then St. Patrick with the approbation of the joint committee expurgated them. After St. Patrick had finished his work Ros the bard " put a thread of poetry round it," that is, drew it all up in verse, so that it might be the better remembered, —a very antique trait indeed—and it is a remarkable proof of the great antiquity of the Brehon Laws that many parts of them, though printed as prose, might be read as poetry, not the poetry of 8th century schools, but a much older unrhymed rhythmical sort of chant which I believe—and have elsewhere tried to prove—was the precursor of the regular metres in Erin. This is the account which has come down to us prefixed to the oldest copies of the Laws, but how much of it is truth and how much fiction I shall not try to determine.

Columkille was also a poet. Poetry seems in fact to have run in the blood of the Irish, both saints and sinners, from the very earliest days until they

lost their language. The great Columkille was
even a bard of renown, and took himself such interest
in the bardic order that had it not been for his
very active interposition at Druim-Ceat they would
have fared badly indeed at the hands of the in-
furiated nobles and kings, whom they had so long
made their prey. This story of how he saved our
bards belongs to Irish history and is too well-known
to need recital. Besides the celebrated Latin hymn
called the "Altus" and others, Columkille is said
to have composed quite a quantity of Irish poems.
Of course it is very hard to tell how many of
the pieces ascribed to him are really his. Many of
them are evidently not the saint's work at all, but
others may very well have been so, though of course
much modified in transcription.

Columkille like Ossian and the Pagan Irish, was
enthusiastically alive to the beauty of Nature. If
—apart from form—there is one distinguishing note
more than another, peculiar to the literature of the
ancient—and to some extent of the modern—Gael,
it is his fondness for Nature in its various aspects.
He seems at times to have been perfectly intoxi-
cated with the mere pleasure of sensations derived
from scenery. Here, for instance, is one of Columkille's poems which may very well be genuine. I
have ventured to translate it into something like
the original metre.

COLUMKILLE, *cecinit.*

Oh Son of my God, what a pride what a pleasure
    To plough the blue sea,
The waves of the fountain of deluge to measure
    Dear Éire to thee.

We are rounding Moy-n-Olurg, we sweep by its
     head and
  We plunge through Loch Foyle,
Whose swans could enchant with their music the
     dead and
  Make pleasure of toil.

The host of the gulls with a joyous commotion
    And screaming and sport
Will welcome my own " Dewy Red " * from the ocean
    Arriving in port.

Oh Erin, were wealth my desire, what a wealth were
    To gain far from thee,
In the land of the stranger, but there even health were
    A sickness to me !

Alas for the voyage, oh high King of Heaven,
    Enjoined upon me,
For that I on the red plain of bloody Cooldrevin †
    Was present to see.

* The name of Columkille's boat. The original runs thus,
modernized—I do not well understand the last words of the third
line :—

      Sluaġ na bhṗaoileán ꝺo buꝺh ṗáilꞇeach
        Re ṛeinm ṛúnꞇach
     Ꝺá ṛoiṛiꞇ roṛꞇ na ṛearṡ ṗáilꞇach
      CCn Ꝺearṡ-Ꝺṛúchꞇach.

† Better Anglicised Cooldrevna. This of course was the well-
known battle field where Columkille and the Ulster men fought
it out with the High King, after his quarrel about copying the
book. The penance enjoined on him by St. Moleesha of Aham-
lish, was that he should leave Ireland and convert as many souls
as there were soldiers slain at this battle. Hence his voyage to
I-Columkille or Iona, and the great monastery he established
there.

How happy the son is of Dima * ; no sorrow
    For him is designed,
He is having, this hour, round his own kill in Durrow
    The wish of his mind.

The sound of the wind in the elms, like the strings of
    A harp being played,
The note of the blackbird that claps with the wings of
    Delight in the glade.

With him in Ros-Grencha the cattle are lowing
    At earliest dawn,
On the " brink of the summer " † the pigeons are
    cooing
    And doves in the lawn.

Three things am I leaving behind me, the very
    Most dear that I know,
Tir-Leedach I'm leaving, and Durrow and Derry,
    Alas I must go !

Yet my visit and feasting with Comgall have eased
    me
    At Cainneach's right hand,
And all but thy Government Erin has pleased me,
    Thou waterfall land.

No doubt many a one has since echoed and echoes
to-day in his own mind these last two lines ; but
in many things Columkille has always appeared to
me from what we know of him—and that is a

* *I.e.*, Cormac O'Liathain, the voyager.
† This is the literal translation of the original, αρ bﬁρυαch
ρamhραιﬁ.

good deal, for we have his life in four books written within a hundred years after his death by Adamnan one of his successors—to have been both in his failings and his virtues the most typical of Irishmen, at once sentimental and impulsive, an eminent type of the race he came from. The story of him and the heron is suggestive in its sentimental tenderness. Because he saw the bird flying across the water from the direction of Ireland and alighting half frozen with cold and faint with flight upon the rocky coast of Iona, he sent out one of his monks to go round the island and warm and cherish and feed the bird, "because," said he, weeping, "it has come from the land I shall never see on earth again." We see his extreme tenderness and love of Nature in all his poems, particularly in a long one beginning "Delightful to be on Ben Edar," the Hill of Howth, some verses of which I may thus translate :—

Delightful it is on Ben Edar to rest,
　　Before going over the white white sea,
The dash of the wave as it launches its crest
　　On the wind-beaten shore is delight to me.*

Delightful it is on Ben Edar to rest
　　When one has come over the white sea foam
His coracle cleaving her way to the west,
　　Through the sport of the waves as she beats
　　　for home.

---

* Literally :—Delightful to be on Ben Edar, before going over the sea, white white, the dashing of the wave against its face. The bareness of the shore and its border.

But now his coracle was not on its way to the
west but to the east, he is leaving, not approaching Erin :—

How swiftly we travel! there is a grey eye
    Looks back upon Erin, but it no more
Shall see while the stars shall endure in the sky,
    Her women, her men, or her stainless shore.

From the plank of the oak where in sorrow I lie
    I am straining my sight through the water and
      wind,
And large is the tear from the soft grey eye
    Looking back on the land that it leaves behind.

How different is the land he is forced to leave
from that to which he must now betake him; he
is going to meet sickness, famine and flint-hearted
men, ah! how different is the western isle he leaves
behind him.

For oh! in the west now the apple is fair!
    How many a Tanist, how many a king;
How many a sloe does the thorn tree bear,
    In the acorned oaks how the young birds sing!

Melodious her clerics, melodious her birds,
    Her children are gentle, her seniors wise,
Her men are illustrious, truthful in words,
    Her women have virtues for love to prize.

He is the first example of the exiled Irishman
grieving for his native land and refusing to be
comforted, "deóraidhthe," as John O'Mahony, when

in New York, touchingly quoted or perhaps composed—

Deopaíohche ʒan ɼʒích ʒan ɼoɼ
Mıanaıo a oʈíɼ 'ɼ a nʼoúʈhchaɼ.*

In far off lands his love for his fellow Gael is as hot, and his desire to return to his native soil as poignant as that of the Fenian leader himself.

I give thee my blessing to carry fair youth,
    And my benediction over the sea,
One sevenfold-half upon Erin in truth,
    One half upon Alba the same to be.

To the nobles who gem the bright isle of the Gael
    Carry this benediction over the sea,
And bid them not credit Moleesha's tale
    And bid them not credit his words of me.

Were it not for the words of Moleesha's mouth
    At the cross of Ahamlish, that sorrowful day,
I now should be warding from north and from south
    Disease and distemper from Erin away.

Then take thee my blessing with thee to the west,
    For my heart in my bosom is broken ; I fail ;
Should death of a sudden now pierce my breast
    I should die of the love that I bear the Gael.

Saint Brigid, the third patron saint of Ireland, is said to have also written verses, with a rule for

* Exiles without rest or respite they long for their country and their patrimony.

her nuns, and some other things.   There certainly
is an antique semi-barbarous air about her poem
beginning :—

> I should like a great lake of ale
> For the king of the kings,
> I should like the family of heaven
> To be drinking it through time eternal, etc.

The Irish saints produced also a great number
of Latin hymns, the oldest of which is that of
Secundinus or Seachnall, a monk of foreign origin
who came to help St. Patrick.   St. Fiacc's metrical
Life of St. Patrick, a poem of seventy lines, is, perhaps, after the Deer's Cry, the oldest bit of Irish
religious verse existing, for Fiacc was St. Patrick's
pupil.   Zimmer considers about half of this poem
genuine; Thurneysen, however,—because it does not
agree with his theory of Irish metric—rejects it.

A great many ancient lives of the early saints
were written, chiefly written in Latin, by their successors, as the Life of St. Patrick ascribed to his disciple
St. Benignus, another to St. Ultan in Ardbraccan,
another to St. Eleran in the sixth century, Tire-
chan's life in the *Book of Armagh,* and the Tri-
partite Life.   Adamnan's Life of Columkille; a Life
of St. Brigit attributed to St. Ultan, and a life
of her written in Latin hexameters by one Caelan
—all these are worthy of mention.   One of the most
voluminous Irish lives is that of St. Columkille composed in Irish in 1532, at the command of Manus
O'Donnell, prince of Tirconnell, at the town now
called Lifford, which gives the contents of all the
old Latin and Irish lives which the compilers
could lay their hands upon.

The Voyage of St. Brendan—who was born in 483—is another remarkable book in its way, which was at one time celebrated over Europe. The saint was certainly a great traveller, as the numerous places called after him all along the coast of Ireland and the west coast of Scotland, as far as lone St. Kilda, show. The celebrated *Navigatio St. Brendani* was probably founded upon some actual tradition, which was built up into a wildly fictitious romance in the seventh or eight century after the fashion dear to the heart of Hibernian authors of that age. It is not now found in Irish, but the 9th century MS. in the Vatican Library at Rome is said to be evidently a literal translation from the Gaelic. The *Voyage of Maeldune* and the *Voyage of the O'Corras* are other popular specimens of this kind of literature, the substance of the first being evidently Pagan, and the latter probably dating from the eleventh century.

The great colleges and monasteries of Moville, in Donegal, founded by St. Finian, " the tutor of the saints of Ireland," the same who quarrelled with Columkille about the famous book ; the school at Clonard in Meath ; the school of St. Enda in Aran ; Clonmacnois, founded by St. Kieran ; the schools of Rahan and Lismore ; St. Kevin's school of Glendalough ; St. Molaise's or Moleesha's school at Devenish island in Loch Erne—it was he who pronounced St. Columkille's banishment ; St. Moling's school at Carlow ; St. Fechin's at Fore, etc., were, outside the bardic colleges, the principal teaching institutions in the sixth, seventh and eighth centuries.

The ninth, tenth and eleventh centuries were not as productive of Christian literature as might have been expected, partly because of the mania for emigration and missionary work which had at that time so seized upon all the best minds of the Gael, and still more on account of the Danish ravages which had thoroughly disorganized the entire nation. It was during these centuries that the Culdees* flourished. They, too, had a number of institutions throughout the island of which that at Tallaght near Dublin is one of the best known. It was here Angus the Culdee (after much solitary preparation in the wilds called after him to-day Disert-Enos† or Angus's desert) entered in the latter half of the 8th century and produced in time his great " Féilïrè " or Calendar. In this work a stanza is given to each day of the year, in connection with some saint—and wherever possible with some Irish saint. It is all written in a short and difficult though melodious metre, here are the beginning stanzas translated exactly into the measure of the original, each six-syllable line ending in a dissyllable :—

* In Irish " Céɪᴌe 'Oé," *i.e.*, Servus Dei, a phrase used with much latitude but in general denoting an ascetic monk, sometimes a missionary one. So far from being pre-Patrician Christians as some have asserted, they seem to be of seventh or eighth century origin. We find the Dominican monks of Sligo called Culdees in a MS. of the year 1600. The Culdees of Scotland having become lax in later times, married and established a kind of spurious hereditary order So much for Campbell's pretty lines in his Reulura :—

> " Peace to their souls, the pure Culdees
>   Were Albyn's earliest priests of God,
> Ere yet an island of her seas
>   By foot of Saxon monk was trod."

† Angus, in Irish Aonghus, is generally pronounced Æneesh, and is sometimes well anglicised " Eneas."

Bless O Christ my speaking
　　King of heavens seven,
Strength and wealth and POWER
　　In this HOUR be *given ;*

Given * O thou brightest
　　Destined not to sever,
King of angels GLORIOUS
　　And VICTORIOUS *ever.*

Ever o'er us shining
　　Light to mortals given,
Beaming daily, NIGHTLY
　　BRIGHTLY out of heaven, etc

The Féiliré is followed by a poem of five or
six hundred lines, and it and the poems connected
with it are perhaps the most extensive specimens of
early Irish poetry which we have. Whitley Stokes,
however, considers them to be of the tenth rather
than the eighth century, which would leave their
authorship doubtful.   It was at Tallaght that Angus
is said to have produced his " Saltair na rann," a poem
of some eight thousand lines, based (like Caedmon's
poems) on Old Testament history, and also the
Martyrology of Tallaght. He died at Clonenagh,
and one of his disciples composed over him that
brief elegy which Matthew Arnold, reading it only in
English, considered so perfectly felicitous in thought

---

* This *tour de force* of beginning each succeeding stanza with
the same word that ends the preceding one, is common in Irish,
where it is called *Conachlonn,* and it is much used by Angus.
Irish prosody is full of original terms unborrowed from Latin,
and to my mind they tell strongly in favour of the theory of a pre-
Christian culture.

and expression. These centuries saw also a number of ecclesiastical documents take form, such as treatises on the Mass, litanies to the Blessed Virgin, and many other litanies, canons (some in verse, as that of Fothadh the Canonist, claiming exemption from military service for clerics, others in prose), hymns, and many other writings, the most valuable of which is beyond doubt the *Book of Hymns* preserved in an eleventh century MS., most of the pieces being indeed in Latin; though with long Irish introductions in prose. The hymns themselves "are unquestionably much older" than the eleventh century, and according to Windisch their language is that of the old Irish glosses in Milan and Würzburg which Zeuss took for the foundation of his *Grammatica Celtica*.

CHAPTER XIV.

THE DANISH PERIOD.

HE first onfall of the Danes
seems to have been made
about the year 795, and
for considerably over two
centuries Erin was shaken
from shore to shore with
ever-recurring alarms, and
for many years every centre
of population lived in a state of terror, not knowing
what a day might bring forth.   Monasteries and
colleges were burnt, numbers of invaluable books
were destroyed, gold and silver work carried off,
and a state of unrest produced which must have
made learning in many parts of the island well-nigh
impossible.

It is probably owing to our round towers that even
so much of the past has been preserved to us.   It
appears to be now pretty well agreed upon that
many of these towers were built as places of refuge
where men, women, and valuables might be saved

from the early incursions of the Danes, who, in their rapid marches from the sea coast to raid the land, could not sit down long enough in front of these stone piles to reduce them, lest the country should be roused in the meantime and the retreat to their ships cut off.

Strange to say, despite the troubled condition of Ireland during these two or three centuries, she produced a large number of poets and scholars, the impulse of the enthusiasm of the sixth and seventh centuries being still strong upon her. Unquestionably the greatest name amongst her men of learning during this period was that of the statesman, ecclesiastic, poet and scholar, Cormac mac Culenan, who was at once King and Bishop of Cashel,* and one of the most striking figures in both the literary and political history of those centuries.

To him we owe that most valuable relic of antiquity called Cormac's Glossary, by far the oldest attempt at a vernacular dictionary made in any language of modern Europe. Of course it has been enlarged by subsequent writers, but the idea and much of the matter remains Cormac's. In its original conception it was meant to explain and elucidate words and phrases which in the ninth century had become obscure to Irish scholars, and, as might be expected, it throws light on many Pagan customs, on history, law, romance and mythology. Cormac's other great work was the compilation of the *Saltair of Cashel*, now most unhappily lost, but it appears to have been a great work. In it was contained

---

* In Irish "Mac Chuileannáin;" it was not he, however, who built Cormac's Chapel at Cashel, but Cormac MacCarthy, in the twelfth century.

he *Book of Rights* drawn up for the readjustment
of the relations existing between princes and tribes, a
book still preserved. St. Benignus was said to have
originally composed in verse a complete statement
of the various rights, privileges and duties of the
High King, the provincial kings, and the local chieftains. This, like all our ancient and primitive laws, was
drawn up in verse so as to be thus stereotyped
for the future, and easily remembered at a time
when books were scarce. Cormac seems to have
enlarged, modified and brought it up to date, to
suit the changing times, and it was subsequently
redacted again in Brian Boramha's (Boru's) day, in
a sense favourable to Munster.

The King-Bishop was at once a remarkable man
and a distinguished scholar. He appears to have
known Latin, Greek, Hebrew and Danish, and to
have been one of the finest Old-Gaelic scholars
of his day, and withal an accomplished poet.
He was slain in battle in the year 908 * under
circumstances so curiously described in the fragmentary annals edited by O'Donovan, that it may
be worth repeating here. He was, as we know
from other sources, betrothed to the Princess
Gormfhlaith or Gormly, daughter of Flann Sionna
King of Meath and High King of Ireland, but
determining to enter the Church he returned her
with her dowry to her father without consummating
the marriage; after which he took orders, and rose
in time to be Archbishop of Cashel as well as
King of Munster. It was in the year 908 that
Gormly was married against her will to Cearbhall
Carroll], King of Leinster. Flann the High King,

* In 903, according to the Four Masters, who, however, at this
period antedate by five years.

with Carroll King of Leinster, now his son-in law, prepared to meet Munster and to assert by arms his
right to the presentation of the ancient church of
Monasterevan, but in reality it is likely that he
bore the King-Archbishop a grudge for his treatment of his daughter Gormly.   Here is the annalistic account of the sequel—it may remind the
classical reader a little of the death of Cyrus.

Death of Cormac mac Cullinan.*

"The great host of Munster was assembled by
the same two, that is Flaherty † [abbot of Mis-Cathaigh,
now Scattery (!) Island on the Shannon] and Cormac
[Mac Cullinan] to demand hostages of Leinster and
Ossory, and all the men of Munster were in the same
camp. . . . And noble ambassadors came from Leinster from Carroll son of Muirigan [king of that province]
to Cormac first, and they delivered a message of
peace from the Leinstermen, *i.e.*, one peace to be
in all Erin until May following (it being then the
second week in autumn), and to give hostages into
the keeping of Maenach, a holy, wise and pious
man, and of other pious men, and to give jewels
and much property to Cormac and Flaherty.

"Cormac was much rejoiced at being offered this
peace, and he afterwards went to tell it to Flaherty

---

* From the fragment copied by Duald mac Firbis in 1643 from
a vellum MS. of Mac Eagan of Ormond, a chief professor of the
old Brehon Law, a MS. which was so worn as to be in places
illegible at the time Mac Firbis copied it ; published by
O'Donovan for the Archæological Society.   I have altered
O'Donovan's translation very slightly.

† *In Irish* "Ⱇlaⱅhbheaⱃⱅach."   He was taken prisoner in
the battle, but released after about a year, having suffered nothing worse than "great abuse from the clergy of Leinster," and
subsequently became King of Munster himself, and reigned for
32 years.

and how he was offered it from Leinster. When Flaherty heard this he was greatly horrified, and 'twas what he said, 'this shows,' said he, 'the littleness of thy mind and the feebleness of thy nature, for thou art the son of a plebeian,' and he said many other bitter and insulting words which it would be too long to repeat.

"The answer which Cormac made him was, 'I am certain,' Cormac said, 'of what the result of this [obstinacy of yours] will be, a battle will be fought, O holy man,' said he, 'and [I] Cormac shall be under a curse for it, and it is likely that it will be the cause of death to thee [also].' And when he had said this he came into his own tent afflicted and sorrowful. And when he sat down he took a basketful of apples and proceeded to divide them amongst his people and said: 'my dear people,' he said, 'I shall never give you apples again from this out for ever.' 'Is it so, O dear earthly lord,' said his people, 'why art thou sorrowful and melancholy with us; it is often thou hast boded evil for us.' 'It is' [said Cormac] 'as I say, and yet dear people what melancholy thing have I said, for though I should not distribute apples to you with my own hand, yet there shall be some one of you in my place who shall.' He afterwards ordered a watch to be set, and he called to him the holy, pious and wise man, Maenach, son of Siadhal [Shiel] the chief co-arb or successor of Comhghall, and he made his confession and will in his presence, and he took the body of Christ from his hand, and he resigned the world in the presence of Maenach, for he knew that he would be killed in battle, but he did not wish that many others should know it. He also ordered that his body should be brought to Cloyne if convenient, but if not, to convey it to the cemetery of Diarmuid [grand] son of Aedh Roin where he had studied for a long time. He was very desirous, however, of being interred at Cloyne of Mac Lenin. Maenach, however, was better pleased to have him interred at Disert-Diarmada for that was one of [Saint] Comhghall's towns, and Maenach was Comhghall's successor. This Maenach, son of Shiel, was the wisest man of his time, and he now exerted himself much, to make peace, if it were possible, between the men of Leinster and Munster.

"Many of the forces of Munster deserted unrestrained. There was great noise too, and dissension in the camp of the men of Munster at this time, for they heard that Flann, son of Malachy* [High King of Ireland] was in the camp of the Leinster men [helping them] with great forces of foot and horse. It was then Maenach said, 'good men of Munster' said he, 'you ought to accept of the good hostages I have offered you to be placed in the custody of pious men till May next, namely, the son of Carroll King of Leinster, and the son of the King of Ossory.' All the men of Munster were saying that it was Flaherty [the abbot] son of Ionmainén alone, who compelled them to go [to fight] into Leinster.

"After this great complaint which they made, they came over Slieve Mairgé from the west to Leithghlinn Bridge. But Tibraide, successor of Ailbhé [of Emly], and many of the clergy along with him, tarried at Leithghlinn, and also the servants of the army and the horses that carried the provisions.

* _In Irish_ "Maoilṛheachlann," pronounced "Mweelhauchlin," but generally contracted to "M'Lauchlin."

"After this trumpets were blown and signals for battle were given by the men of Munster, and they went forwards till they came to Moy-Ailbhé.* Here they remained with their back to a thick wood awaiting their enemies. The men of Munster divided themselves into three equally large battalions, Flaherty son of Ionmainen and Ceallach son of Cearbhall [Carroll], King of Ossory, over the first division, Cormac mac Cullenan, King of Munster, over the middle division, Cormac son of Mothla, King of the Deisi, and the King of Kerry and the kings of many other tribes of West Munster over the third division. They afterwards came on in this order to Moy-Ailbhé. They were querulous on account of the numbers of the enemy, and their own fewness. Those who were knowledgeable, that is, those who were amongst themselves, state that the Leinstermen and their forces amounted to three times or four times the number of the men of Munster or more. Unsteady was the order in which the men of Munster came to the battle. Very pitiful was the wailing which was in the battle, as the learned who were in the battle relate—the shrieks of the one host in the act of being slaughtered, and the shouts of the other host exulting over that slaughter. There were two causes for which the men of Munster suffered so sudden a defeat; for Céileachar the brother of Cingégan suddenly mounted his horse and said, 'nobles of Munster,' said he, 'fly suddenly from this abominable battle, and leave it between the clergy themselves, who could not be quiet without coming to battle,' and afterwards he suddenly fled

* The plain where this battle of Bealach Múghna or Ballaghmoon was fought, is in the very south of the County Kildare, about 2½ miles to the north of the town of Carlow.

accompanied by great hosts. The other cause of
the defeat was: when Ceallach son of Carroll saw
the battalion in which were the chieftains of the
king of Erin cutting down his own battalion, he
mounted his horse and said to his own people,
'mount your horses and drive the enemy before
you.'   And though he said this, it was not to
really fight he said so, but to fly. Howsoever
it resulted from these causes that the Munster
battalions fled together. Alas! pitiful and great
was the slaughter throughout Moy-Ailbhé afterwards.
A cleric was not spared more than a layman,
there they were all equally killed. When a
layman or a clergyman was spared it was not
out of mercy it was done, but out of covetousness,
to obtain a ransom from him, or to bring him
into servitude. King Cormac, however, escaped
in the van of the first battalion, but his horse
leaped into a trench and he fell off it. When a
party of his people who were flying perceived this,
they came to the king and put him up on his
horse again.   It was then he saw a foster son of
his own, a noble of the Eoghanachts, Aedh by name,
who was an adept in wisdom and pious prudence
and history and Latin, and the king said to him,
'beloved son,' said he, 'do not cling by me but
take thyself out of it as well as thou canst; I
told thee before, that I should be killed in this
battle.'   A few remained with Cormac, and he
came forward along the way on horseback, and
the road was besmeared throughout with much
blood of men and horses. The hind feet of his
horse slipped on the slippery way in the track of
blood, and the horse fell right back and [Cormac's]
back and neck were both broken, and he said

when falling 'In manus tuas, domine, commendo spiritum meum,' and he gave up the ghost ; and the impious sons of malediction came and thrust spears through his body and cut off his head.

"Although much was the slaying on Moy-Ailbhé to the east of the Barrow, yet the prowess of Leinster was not satisfied with it, but they followed up the rout westwards across Slieve-Mairgé, and slew many noblemen in that pursuit.

"In the very beginning of the battle Ceallach son of Carroll King of Ossory, and his son were killed at once. Dispersedly, however, others were killed from that out, both laity and clergy. There were many good clergymen killed in this battle as were also many kings and chieftains. In it was slain Fogartach, son of Suibhne [Sweeney], an adept in philosophy and divinity, King of Kerry, and Ailell, son of Eóghan (Owen), the distinguished young sage and high-born nobleman, and Colman, abbot of Cenn-Etigh, chief ollav of the judicature of Erin, and hosts of others also, quos largum est scribere. . . .

"Then a party came up to Flann, having the head of Cormac with them, and 'twas what they said to Flann, 'Life and health O powerful victorious king, and Cormac's head to thee from us, and as is customary with kings, raise thy thigh and put this head under it, and press it with thy thigh.' Howsoever, Flann spoke evil to them, it was not thanks he gave them. 'It was an awful act,' said he, 'to have taken off the head of the holy bishop, but, however, I shall honour it instead of crushing it.' Flann took the head into his hand and kissed it and carried thrice round him the consecrated head of the holy bishop and true martyr. The head was afterwards honourably

carried away from him to the body where Maenach
son of Siadhal [Shiel] successor of Comhghall was,
and he carried the body of Cormac to Castledermot
where it was honourably interred, and where it per-
forms signs and miracles.

"Why should not the heart repine and the mind
sicken at this enormous deed, the killing and the
mangling with horrid arms of this holy man, the
most learned of all who came or shall come of the
men of Erin for ever. The complete master of
Gaedhlic and Latin, the archbishop most pious
most pure, miraculous in chastity and prayer, a
proficient in law and in every wisdom, knowledge,
and science, a paragon of poetry and learning, a
head of charity and every virtue, a sage of education, and head-king of the whole of the two Munster
provinces in his time!"

Gormly the betrothed, but afterwards repudiated
bride of Cormac, was also a poet, and there are
many pieces ascribed to her. She was, as I mentioned, married to Carroll, King of Leinster, who was
severely wounded in this battle. He was carried
home to be cured in his palace at Naas, and Gormly,
the queen, was constant in her attendance on him.
One day, however, as Carroll was becoming convales-
cent he fell to exulting over the mutilation of Cormac
at which he had been present. The queen, who was
sitting at the foot of his bed, rebuked him for it, and said
that the body of a good man had been most unworthily
desecrated. At this Carroll, who was still confined to
bed, became angry and kicked her over with his foot
in the presence of all her attendants and ladies.

As her father the High King would do nothing
for her, when she besought him to wipe out the

insult and procure her separation from her husband, her young kinsman, Niall Glún-dubh or the Black-kneed, took up her cause, and obtained for her a divorce from her husband, and restoration of her dowry. When her husband was killed by the Danes, the year after that, she married Niall, who in time succeeded to the throne as High King of all Ireland, and who was one of the noblest of Irish monarchs. He, too, was finally slain by the Danes,* and the monarchy passed away from the houses both of her father and her husband, and she, the daughter of one High King, the wife of another, bewails in her old age the poverty and neglect into which she had fallen. She dreamt one night that King Niall stood beside her, and she made a leap forwards to clasp him in her arms, but struck herself against the bed-post, and received a wound from which she never recovered. Many of her poems are lamentations on her kinsman and husband Niall. They seem to have been popular amongst the Highland as well as the Irish Gaels. Here is a specimen jotted down in phonetic spelling by the Scotch Dean Macgregor, about the year 1512.

> Take grey monk thy foot away,
>   Lift it off the grave of Neill;
> Too long thou heapest up the clay,
>   O'er him who cannot feel.†

* King Niall is scarely yet forgotten. This very year the Celtic Literary Society of Dublin, organized a pilgrimage to his grave on Tibradden Mountain in that county.

† The first verse runs thus in modern Gaelic :—

> beir a mhanaigh leat do chor
>   Tóg anoir i de thaoibh Néill,
> Ir rómhór chuirir do chró
>   Ar an té le luidhinn féin.

See p. 75 of the Gaelic part of the *Book of the Dean of Lismore.*

Monk, why must thou pile the earth
   O'er the couch of noble Neill,
Above my friend of gentle birth
   Thou strik'st thy churlish heel

Leave his clay unpressed to-night,
   Mournful monk of saddest voice ;
Beneath it lies my heart's delight
   Who made me to rejoice.

Monk, remove thy foot, I say,
   Tread not on the sacred ground
Where Neill is shut from me away
   In cold and narrow bound.

I am Gormly—king of men
   Was my father, Flann the brave ;
I charge thee stand thou not again,
   Bold monk upon his grave.

Some other poets of great note flourished in
Ireland in the tenth and eleventh centuries, such
as Cormac "an Eigeas" who composed the celebrated poem to Muircheartach or Murtagh of the
leather cloaks* (son of the Niall so bitterly lamented by Gormly), on the occasion of his marching
round Ireland, when setting out from his palace at
ancient Oileach he returned to it again after levy-
ing tribute and receiving hostages from every king
and sub-king in Ireland.   This great O'Neill well
deserved a poet's praise, for having taken Sitric,
the Danish lord of Dublin, Ceallachan of Munster,
the King of Leinster, and the royal heir of Connacht
as hostages, he, understanding well that in the inter-
ests of Ireland the High Kingship should be upheld,
positively refused to follow the advice of his own

* ⁊ɼⱺ ᵹᵓᵓᵓᵕᶜᴵⱼⱥᶫ ᴄⱼⱺⱼᶜⱼᵓⱼⱼ.

clan and march, as they urged, on Tara to take hostages from Donagh the High King. On the contrary, he actually sent of his own accord all those that had been given him during his circuit to Donagh as supreme monarch of Ireland. He, on his part, not to be out-done in magnanimity, returned them again to Murtagh with the message that he into whose hands they had been delivered, was the proper person to keep them. It was to commemorate this that Cormac wrote his poem of 256 lines, beginning

> CC Mhuiṗcheaṗtaiġh Mheic Néill náiṗ
> Ro ġabhaiṡ ġialla Inṗe-Ḟáil.*

But the names of the poets Cinaeth or Kenneth O'Hartigan and Eochaidh O'Flynn are the most celebrated amongst those of the tenth century. Allusions to and quotations from the first, who died in 975 are frequent, and nine or ten of his poems have been preserved perfect for us. Of O'Flynn's pieces fourteen are enumerated by O'Reilly, containing in the aggregate between seventeen and eighteen hundred lines. In them we find in verse the whole early and mythical history of Ireland. We have for instance one poem on the invasion of Partholan, and on the invasion of the Fomorians, another on the division of Ireland between the sons of Partholan, another on the destruction of the tower of Conaing and the battles between the Fomorians and Nemedians, another on the journey of the Nemedians from Scithia and how some emigrated to Greece and others to Britain after the destruction of Conaing's tower, another on the invasion of the sons of Milesius, another on the

---

* O Muircheartach son of noble Niall,
Thou hast taken hostages of Inisfail.

history of Emania built by Cimbaeth some 300 years before Christ, up to its destruction by the three Collas in the year 331. This poet in especial may be said to have crystallised into verse the mythic history of Ireland with the names and reigns of the Irish kings, and to have thrown them into the form of real history, but whether all that he relates had taken solid shape and form before he versified it anew, or whether, as some imagine, he was really the first to collect the floating tribe-legends and race myths, and cast them into the historical shape in which later annalists record them, by fitting them into a complete scheme of genealogical history like that of the Old Testament, is a question which it is hard at present to decide.

About this time too lived Mac Liag, who was Brian Boru's secretary, and who is said—erroneously according to O'Curry—to have written a life of Brian Boru, and an account of the wars of Brian in Munster, along with a number of poems. His name will be remembered through Mangan's beautiful translation of his address to Kincora the seat of Brian's palace.

Oh where, Kincora, is Brian the great,
    And where is the beauty that once was thine,
Oh where are the princes and nobles that sate
    To feast in thy halls and drink the red wine,
                Where, O Kincora?

·   ·   ·   ·   ·   ·   ·   ·

They are gone, those heroes of royal birth,
    Who plundered no churches, who broke no trust;
'Tis weary for me to be living on earth,
    When they, O Kincora, lie low in the dust,
                Low, O Kincora.

During all this period the bardic colleges were not neglected, but continued to flourish as before, and to cultivate side by side law, history, and poetry. The prosody of the Irish language as reduced to form, and taught by the ollavs, was something unique and wonderful, nearly three hundred different metres being recognized and practised.

To give any adequate account of these bardic schools and of the course pursued in them, is unfortunately impossible within the brief space at my disposal for this short story of our early literature. That story I have, roughly speaking, brought down to the Danish Period, overlapping it indeed—from the necessity of the case—in more than one chapter. I may now take farewell of my readers in a few verses which may serve as a specimen of one of the best-known metres, indeed the great official one, of the Irish bards, the celebrated Deibhidh* [D'yevvee]. This metre, with all the other artificial measures of the schools, was lost in the seventeenth or eighteenth century, and these lines are the first composed in it, in either Irish or English, for over 150 years :—

* The following are the requirements of the above metre, requirements which were pretty rigorously observed by the bards in later times, though I think some of the points were not reduced to rigid rule as early as the Danish period. There are four lines in each *rann*, seven syllables in each line, two or more alliterations of accented syllables in each line, the word which ends the second and fourth lines must have a syllable more than that which ends the first and third. If the accent falls on the ultimate syllable of the first and third lines it must fall on the penult of the second and fourth, if on the penultimate of the first and third, it must fall on the antepenultimate of the second and fourth. There must be *co-arda* or Irish rhyme between the last words of the first and second lines, and the third and fourth, but the third and fourth also require Irish-rhyme between two or more words in the middle of the line.

Bound thee forth my Booklet quíck
To greet the Polished Públic.
Writ—I *WEEN*'t was not my Wísh—
In *LEAN* unLovely Énglish.

Tell of ancient Times and mén
(The Tale is Told not óften)
And to-D*A Y* the Dust lies thíck
On Learnèd L*A Y* and Lýric.

Speak the deeds of Famous Fínn
Of Con and of Cu-chúlain
Tales of T*IME* recorded áll
In Rann and R*HYME* and ánnal.

Cairbrè Killed among his mén
The Fenian Fall so súdden,
OSSIAN from his Seat of Sóng
By *FASHION* Hurlèd Heádlong.

All unWot of now, I Wís
Our Ancient Epic ríches,
Yet are S*EEN*, though S*AD* and síck
Some G*LAD* to G*LEAN* a rélic.

Glad to Glean a relic, Í,
Though Mock'd I be by Mány,
Take my T*ALE* to stranger men
The G*AEL* the Gael is fállen.

CRIOCH.

www.ingramcontent.com/pod-product-compliance
Lightning Source LLC
Chambersburg PA
CBHW030543040726
47497CB00008B/2564